The
Plucker

More from D.K. Cassidy

Spilt Milk: A Collection of Stories
Curious Reality

The Plucker

D.K. Cassidy

The Plucker
Copyright © 2016 by D.K. Cassidy

This is a fictional story. The events, names, and characters are fictitious, and any similarity to real persons, living or dead, or actual events are purely coincidental.

ISBN: 978-1-941938-03-4
Library of Congress Control Number: 2016949472

Pluvio
press

Editing: Crystal Watanabe Pikkoshouse.com
Cover Design: Designforwriters.com
Interior Design: NovelNinjutsu.com

Contents

Dedication

I dedicate this book to my husband Mark,
my sons Aidan and Jared,
and to my sisters Joan and Fran.

Thank you for your continued love and support.

Chapter One

Just one more.

Okay, another one.

Pria couldn't help herself. She didn't want to stop.

Well, if I pluck one more on each side they'll be even.

She loved to pluck her eyebrows every other Sunday. Gathering the plucked hairs with meticulous care, Pria placed them in a Mason jar. The short black hairs came up to the word 'Mason' stamped on the lower half of the jar. Her goal: to fill it. Not sure why. Not sure she needed a reason other than the achievement she felt. The warm glow of joy. The shiver of pleasure. The excitement of having a secret.

Goals: an objective her parents talked about. Not something she aspired to until now. This goal seemed worthy of her efforts. She could be proud of this

1

achievement. A secret goal for her to attain. No one would know; it didn't matter. No one to impress.

Pria knew her parents wouldn't be proud of her for this goal. They would feel horrified. Shocked. Ashamed.

Looking in the mirror once again, she willed herself to leave her eyebrows alone. Her right hand began to tremble then crept up to the back of her head. If she couldn't pluck her eyebrows, the hair on her head would serve as a worthy substitute. Her scalp began to tingle in anticipation, her body trained to enjoy her attention.

Lifting her long hair, Pria wound a black strand around her forefinger. Tugging gently, she felt herself shudder. Increasing the pressure doubled the pleasure. Anticipating the release of tension, she yanked the strand of hair free from her scalp. Pria released her breath and relaxed.

It felt better than any description of sex she'd read.

Pria remembered her childhood, when her worried mother took her to a psychiatrist to find out why her little girl kept pulling on her eyebrows. Her mother and the doctor didn't know that Pria also pulled out her hair when she was alone. There were little bald patches at the base of her skull. She kept this secret by not allowing her mother to brush her hair.

She insisted that at eight years old she was a big girl and didn't need help.

Her mother felt proud of her daughter's independence, fooled by the ruse. Never guessing Pria's secret activity. Or never allowing herself to suspect her daughter of anything not as it should be. She was their only child, her existence bordered on miraculous. They weren't able to have any other children. She was a gift, perfect in the filtered vision of a mother.

Every morning before she left for school, Pria braided her long hair. She arranged the top layer to hide the growing bald patch underneath. As the patch grew, she began to wear a headband. Lucky for her, these were a common accessory for little girls. Headbands were another way for an unusual girl to blend in, part of a sea of regular girls all with bright pieces of cloth tied around their heads.

Individuality achieved through conformity within a homogeneous group.

Hoping to fit in, she chose the most popular headband colors and designs, begging her mother to buy them for her. Being different caused Pria anxiety.

She was the only foreign child in their neighborhood and in her school. A speck of brown in a sea of white.

Hers were the only parents who didn't speak perfect English. Hers was the only house that smelled of exotic foods. Hers was the only mother dressed in a sari. They stood out simply by existing. Without conscious effort, her parents shamed Pria.

Pria refused to bring curry in her lunch. She told her mother she would rather starve. This shocked her parents, Ranjeet and Sunita. Pria had always been such a quiet and obedient child. Given the choice between their dear child going hungry or feeding her strange food, the strange food won out. They decided to indulge her by letting her take peanut butter and jelly to school. In secret, they thought the sandwich disgusting, but kept that opinion to themselves. They conspired to keep many of their opinions secret.

Denying Pria anything proved difficult. She had become secretive, worrying Sunita. Concerned about regaining her daughter's confidences, her regular thriftiness gave way to gifts. Dolls, games, or candy, anything to make Pria happy. Anything to pry the secrets stored in her head.

Strange things happened when Pria was unhappy. Things Sunita tried to ignore—broken light bulbs, cracked mirrors. She scoffed at the absurd idea lingering at the back of her thoughts, not willing to make the connection.

Pria remembered the first time she opened her lunch containing an aromatic chicken curry. The other children in the lunchroom looked around, trying to determine what they smelled. Several wrinkled their noses in disgust. Pria slammed her lunchbox shut, forgoing her meal. That was a defining event for her. She would fit in at all costs. Tamping down the hunger pangs gave her a sense of empowerment. Control. A feeling she treasured. A feeling she would become addicted to.

The next day she opened her lunch with pride, the contents completely normal. Completely American. Peanut butter and jelly sandwich. Grapes. Milk. No noses wrinkled. Her bland lunch joined the plain food carried to school by the other students. Pria munched on the sandwich feeling contentment. She took a moment to treasure that rare emotion.

The diagnosis was trichotillomania. Although the psychiatrist explained the condition, Pria's mother needed to look up the word. English was not her native language.

Shock. She learned her daughter's odd behavior was considered a psychological condition. After discovering the meaning of psychological, she felt her face burn with shame. Her daughter could be classified as crazy. *Crazy*. Something no one in her family suffered from. Or at least, no one admitted to. Brushing aside thoughts of an uncle who 'went away,' Sunita knew she would not let the same happen to Pria.

The dictionary defined trichotillomania as 'a self-induced and recurrent loss of hair.'

"Pria, what is wrong with you? Why must you pull on your eyebrows? You look absurd!"

Her mother frowned, her thick black eyebrows threatening to meet. Lips pursed, the wrinkles on her upper lip coexisted with dark fuzz. Grabbing a dark eyeliner pencil, she angrily filled in the gaps in Pria's eyebrows. Pria waited for her mother to finish, not saying anything, ignoring her mother's urgent question.

Her father tutted from his chair. He couldn't understand what was happening to his daughter. Mumbling about *crazy American problems* he returned to his newspaper. He didn't interfere, preferring to let his wife handle the situation.

Ranjeet often hid from domestic issues behind his treasured newspaper, leaving behind the cramped living room. He concentrated on the wafting scent of curry and dreamed of returning to India. Of being home. He still considered his life in America temporary.

This wasn't home. He wanted to return to his village, but couldn't. Not yet. Pria's education came first, according to his wife. He deferred to his wife in all matters relating to Pria. She was, after all, only a girl.

He remembered a time when the only thing for a girl was marriage. Wondering when the world changed, he shook his paper with indignation. Finding his place on the page, he reentered the safe world of ink and paper.

Pria didn't answer but felt her hand twitch, a sign she needed to pluck something. That morning was the first time she noticed string growing out of her arms. Sliding her sleeves down to hide them, Pria wanted to keep this miracle a secret.

When her mother diverted her attention to cleaning the kitchen, Pria walked to her bedroom. She had a few moments before leaving for school; she needed some time alone to inspect her miracle.

There were three strings on her left forearm. Two were light red, one was lavender. Pria used her wooden ruler to measure these delights, each a different length. The longest string was 1mm. She needed to pluck one to get her through the school day. The other two could wait until later in the afternoon. She chose her pointed tweezers for this task. The slanted tweezers were reserved for her eyebrows when she couldn't extract the hair with her fingers.

She experienced relief and a shiver of delight after pulling the lavender string. Pria put her tweezers back into her sock drawer, underneath her purple socks. Time to head to school and see George. Or rather, follow George. Pria didn't have the nerve to talk to him.

I wish I could show George my miracle. He'd understand, but he doesn't know I exist. He's never looked at me. Never said hello. Never asked me to play. But I know he'd understand. I wonder if he has any miracles in his life?

No one else would understand. Not her mother. Not her psychiatrist. Certainly not her father.

As an adult, Pria chose to live alone, her existence full of schedules and rituals. A roommate wouldn't understand her needs and compulsions. Privacy guaranteed her a place to be Pria.

On Mondays, Pria plucked her guitar for exactly twenty-one minutes. No particular tune. She couldn't read music. Plucking the guitar strings one at a time—E, B, G, D, A, E—soothed her. This piece of wood had the power to make her happy. It contained magic, the powerful magic of happiness and contentment.

The guitar held a place of honor in her small apartment. She'd added a shelf above her fireplace to store the guitar, Mason jar, and other collectibles. A clear flower vase held her strings. Different colors appeared on her forearm every day.

She'd looked up her string condition: Morgellons disease. Some doctors thought the disease didn't exist. It disappointed her to read that. Pria glanced up at her vase of strings.

There they are. Proof. The strings are proof I have this disease. My miracle disease. Those doubters should believe and find joy in a miracle. One day I'll reveal this vase and prove the reality of my disease. But I wish it wasn't called that, it makes it sound like something bad, instead of the gift it is to me.

She had all the listed symptoms: itchiness, feeling something crawling under her skin, and the threads, although she referred to them as strings. They either grew out of her skin or were anchored just beneath the surface. The submerged threads she liked best because she had to dig them out with a needle or a fingernail. She kept her fingernails long for this purpose.

She collected her proof patiently, waiting to display it at the perfect time. When her arms began to itch, it delighted her. It meant a new string was growing out of or into her arm. If she was somewhere private, she could pull up her sleeve and gaze at what she still insisted on calling her miracle.

Pria protected her secret by only wearing long-sleeved shirts. All year. Even on the hottest days, when she planned on being out in public she selected a long-sleeved shirt from her cramped closet. Her short-sleeved tops were reserved for the privacy of her apartment. So she could better admire her strings.

She remembered the day she found the guitar in a thrift shop. The price tag said $21. Twenty-one was her favorite number. Pria had no choice, the guitar needed to come home with her. A sign from the Universe. She took twenty-one bills out of her wallet, one dollar at a time, and handed the money to the cashier. She resisted the urge to hug her purchase. A furtive pat would do for now. And a small sigh.

The first evening she owned her new treasure, Pria stared at it. Not sure what to do with the instrument, she placed it next her fireplace knowing she would add a shelf for it above the mantelpiece. During the night, the solution came to her in a dream. Plucking the strings in order would produce a soothing sound. Plucking: the solution to most things in her small life.

The Plucker

She found out the opening notes of a famous Beatles song began with the first six strings of the guitar. If they thought the sound was perfect, so did she. Those notes became her song of life. Pria's song. She and the Beatles loved the same progression of notes. Another reason she felt special.

The guitar became part of her Monday ritual. She'd purchased the guitar on a Monday, the date predetermined for her. The strings from her arm she plucked whenever they appeared; they were not assigned a particular day. They deserved her attention regardless of the day of the week.

Chapter Two

Each day began with her waiting on the corner. She walked near George every morning on her way to school. Too shy to walk next to him, she felt content to be in his vicinity. George emerged from his house with his red backpack slung over both chubby shoulders. He didn't walk to school, he meandered.

Pria was pleased to meander near him.

As Pria approached their elementary school one morning, George stopped, looked around, then opened his backpack. He pulled out a book with pictures of dragons on the cover, staring at it for a moment. He shoved it back into his backpack and grinned.

Pria felt stunned by George's expression. She'd never noticed him grinning, smiling, or looking the least bit happy. He maintained a solemn look on his round face every day. What could account for this drastic change? Could it simply be the book he held?

"Today we will be going on a field trip to the downtown library to get cards."

Mrs. Franks seemed excited to get her kindergarten class their first library cards.

"We'll be leaving after recess, so play hard and get all your wiggles out. Libraries are quiet places."

The excited class began to chatter and giggle. A field trip meant freedom and fun. Friends pledged to stay together in the library, setting up their own duos, unaware Mrs. Franks had other plans for how the students would be grouped.

George picked up his backpack, hugging it to himself. He knew about the library. He'd discovered it a few weeks ago while seeking shelter from the rain. The book in his bag was from there. He'd taken it, not knowing about library cards then.

It didn't feel like stealing. He simply wanted to add it to the collection of treasured items he stored in his closet. His book collection piled at one end of a shelf threatened to topple whenever he entered his haven. The library quickly became his second favorite place.

George's best-loved place remained his closet.

Pria sat on a swing watching the girls play hopscotch. Not good at the game, she preferred to watch and not be teased. The rules confused her and the pressure to throw her marker onto a particular square made her feel queasy. Any type of stress caused her to pluck at her eyebrows, so staying calm became her defense against standing out.

George sat on the ground near his classroom's door. Reading his dragon book helped him shut out the sounds of the other children having fun. Fun. He wasn't sure why they yelled and laughed so loud. If he were that loud at home, his mother would spank him—or worse.

Mrs. Franks watched the two misfits with sadness. She had tried to get them to interact with their classmates, but failed. They each preferred their own company. The only hint that Pria wanted a friend was the way she stared at George. Mrs. Franks tucked that observation away for later use.

After recess the children lined up at the front of the classroom. Mrs. Franks assigned partners for the field trip. Knowing children formed cliques, she placed puzzle segments in a giant fishbowl and had them pull out a piece and match them with another child. There were twenty-five students, so one of them would be paired with the teacher.

George had the odd puzzle piece, so his partner was Mrs. Franks by default. Fitting. He had no friends in class. Not aware of Pria's crush on him, his small world consisted of himself, his cat Milky, and his closet. His mother didn't make it into his circle. She existed just outside of it.

Mrs. Franks told her class to hold hands with their field-trip buddy. Pria grasped Ralph's hand with reluctance. It was clammy and sticky. She tried to pull away but he held on with the tenacity of a bulldog. Pria quelled her feelings of revulsion and walked toward the school bus.

"George, are you excited about going to the library today?" Mrs. Franks attempted again to get George to open up to her.

He nodded, moving his head with a jerky motion.

"Have you ever been to the library?"

George shook his head with almost no discernible motion this time. He didn't want his teacher to know about the stolen book. A lie wasn't a lie unless you said it out loud. Lying out loud always led to pain.

"Well, then you're in for a big treat. Libraries have always been one of my favorite places."

Mrs. Franks gave him her friendliest smile.

George stared at her then looked out the window of the packed bus. He could feel his teacher's eyes on the back of his head, trying to read his thoughts.

The bus pulled up to the library, parking in front. Mrs. Franks clapped her hands three times, her signal to quiet down. The excited children continued bouncing on the torn vinyl bus seats. She clapped again, and this time the children heard and settled down.

"Grab your buddy's hand and line up outside the bus, please."

Mrs. Franks stood at the bottom of the bus' steps, watching her students. There were no parent volunteers today. She realized too late she should have asked for some assistance, chiding herself for being too self-sufficient. A headache began to form between her eyebrows.

"Nathan! Where is your coat? Ralph, don't let go of Pria's hand until I give you permission. Pria, stop trying to pull away from Ralph. George, wait for me."

Three more claps signaled they could begin walking toward the entrance of the library.

Mrs. Stevenson, the head librarian, nodded at the silent kindergarten class as they filed into the meeting room. She decided to corral the children in that room rather than give them the entire library to roam in.

Once they got their cards she and the teacher would guide them to the children's section.

George hung back unnoticed by either woman. He was very good at not being noticed. He wanted to find another book to take; he'd looked at the drawings in the dragon book hundreds of times. It was time to find another book to collect.

Pria raised her hand, waving it urgently until Mrs. Franks noticed.

"Yes, Pria? What's the matter?"

Pria's upraised hand surprised Mrs. Franks. This quiet, shy student never drew attention to herself.

"Mrs. Franks, may I go to the restroom before we get our library cards? I really need to go."

"Okay, that's a good idea. Anyone else need to go?"

Half the class raised their hands.

"Hurry up, the librarian is waiting for us."

Pria raced into the restroom and headed straight for the sink. Not the toilet. Her urgency had nothing to do with that. She needed to wash Ralph off of her hand. The stickiness and sweat he left on her made her queasy. Pria scrubbed her hands until she felt clean again.

While holding them under the dryer she noticed the skin on one of her cuticles. The tiny piece of skin hanging there, waiting to be plucked. She'd never considered her cuticles as plucking opportunities until that morning.

Delighted and excited, Pria decided to wait until after school. She needed to choose the best tool for the job. Tweezers? Manicure scissors? Or should she just twist the piece of skin and pull? So many choices.

"Now, before we go into the main library, let me explain how your new cards work. First, you will tell me and my assistants the following information: your first and last name, your date of birth, your address and phone number, and the names of your parents or guardians. Don't worry if you can't remember everything. Your teacher has the information."

Mrs. Franks held up a sheet of paper for the class to see.

"She wants you to practice talking to me because it's very important you know these things. Everyone ready?" Mrs. Stevenson looked at each child with a solemn but encouraging face.

Once the paperwork was complete, the librarian led the class to the children's section. It was arranged in a semi-circle containing low cushy stools, tables, and short bookcases. The children milled around looking for something interesting. Quiet sounds of joy indicated the discovery of the perfect book. No one had to be hushed, they were all intent on finding a treasure.

The Plucker

Pria checked out two books then waited by the entrance of the library. She kept playing with the bit of skin on her finger. She wondered why the rest of the class was taking so long to decide on what to check out. It was time to get back on the bus, time to finish the day so she could go home.

At last the kindergarteners lined up, ready to leave. Mrs. Franks told them to join hands with their buddies again. Pria was ready this time. She pulled her sleeve over her hand before taking Ralph's sticky one. Ralph didn't notice; he was engrossed in the large book of dinosaurs clutched in his free hand.

George held Mrs. Franks' hand. A small grin on his face, he patted his backpack containing a book with drawings of castles. This was going into his collection. There was just enough room for this last book. After that he'd move on to another interest. No one knew he'd taken it. He'd used his new library card to check out two other books he didn't care about.

Pria looked over at George, wondering why he looked happy. He never looked happy, yet this was the second time today. Confused, she wondered if he was thinking about someone, a friend she didn't know about.

Arriving back at school, the class sat on the floor around their teacher. Each student knew they would be talking about one of the books they'd selected. Both Pria and George dreaded their turn to speak.

Pria couldn't resist the urge to twist off the hanging piece of cuticle, her anxiety rising with the knowledge that she'd have to stand up and talk about her book. She turned and twisted until the minute piece of skin came off in her hand. She slipped the little treasure into her pocket and felt calmer. Now she could do anything. Even speak in front of the other kids.

Mrs. Franks looked around to see who wanted to speak next. For the second time that day she was surprised to see Pria's hand up.

Hmmm... I wonder what's gotten into that child?

"I see that Pria would like to be next. All right Pria, come up to the front, please, and bring one of your books to share with us."

The class turned as one to watch her make her way to the front of the class with care and stand next to the teacher, her book clasped to her chest, her eyes still lowered. Everyone waited with expectation. It was rare to hear her speak.

"The book I am sharing with you is all about the birds of North America."

Pria held up the book, showing her classmates the cover.

The Plucker

"I think it might be something I'd like to read. Anyway, I like this book because it has lots of pictures and tells me about birds. That's all."

After her turn, Pria took her place on the floor, feeling a blush heating her light brown cheeks.

Mrs. Franks noticed George doing his best not to look at her. Trying to decide whether it was better to get him to confront his fear of speaking or let him wait to be last conflicted her. Decision made, she walked to George and tapped him on the shoulder.

"George, would you like to go next?"

A command, not a question.

George closed his eyes and wished he were safe in his closet. He felt his teacher tap him on the shoulder again. He looked up at her face, hoping for a brief reprieve, but saw none. George took a deep breath then made his way to the front. His book was clasped behind him.

Avoiding the faces of the other students, he focused on the world map displayed on the back wall of the kindergarten class. Spotting Antarctica, he focused on it and began to speak in a whisper.

"Well… this is a book all about rocks."

He flashed the book's cover in the general direction of the class.

George's speech was complete. Despite the brevity of his report, his teacher let him stop. He rushed to the back of the classroom, scooting as close as possible against the wall containing his savior: the world map.

Chapter Three

Tuesdays were for plucking up her courage to try new things. This week: riding the bus across town. She plucked exact change out of her purse. The bus driver stared. She saw that; perhaps he was fascinated by her skill. Pluck, pluck, plucking up courage. A rare smile of pride spread across her delicate features.

Walking down the bus aisle Pria noticed a woman deep breathing with gusto. She decided to sit elsewhere. The noisy breathing disturbed her. Was the woman about to faint?

A vacant seat three rows back suited her. Placing her purse beside her to ensure no seat partner, she watched the rest of the passengers. There was no shortage of riders to observe; the bus contained a cross-section of characters.

A suspicious-looking guy with a hoodie sat right in front of her. He kept staring at the woman who was hyperventilating. Pria wondered if they knew each other. During the entire trip he never took his eyes off the older blonde woman. When the woman exited the bus, he watched which direction she walked. Pria shivered, worrying he might be planning to harm that woman.

Not wanting the hoodie guy to follow her, she signaled her stop at the last moment, causing the bus driver to slam on the brakes and swear loudly. She walked off the bus, head down, blushing with shame. No one else got off.

Pria resisted the urge to watch the bus pass, not wanting to know if he watched her. The hoodie guy flinched when the window next to him cracked, forming a spider web of glass. She didn't like to use this power of hers but felt justified in this case. Pria heard the splintering glass and felt relief. Now certain he wouldn't follow her, she slowed her pace.

She'd accomplished today's goal, then chided herself for not planning better. Yes, she took the bus across town, but now what? There was no mall or park at this stop. Not knowing what else to do, she sat on the bench across the street, waiting for a bus to take her back to her apartment.

The Plucker

To pass the time she picked at the bits of string that were peeking out of her arms. Today's strings were blue. She was hoping for red. Not sure why the Thursday strings changed color, Pria felt a bit off kilter. What else would change today?

Idly observing the passing cars, she noticed a large van with a wheelchair icon on the side and the words *Blue Lake Community Pool*. Her eyes moved to the driver and stopped. She kept staring at the driver, not believing her eyes.

No, it can't be. She'd heard he was a computer programmer. At least, he went to school to be one. Why would he be driving a van for work? Maybe he was a volunteer? *He looks the same. Taller, an adult, but still the same round, serious face. The beard looks good on him.*

The driver was her childhood crush, George. She hadn't thought about him for a long time. Once her family moved away from his neighborhood, she'd given up on him. George never noticed her, but in her mind no one ever did. No reason for him to be any different.

The van stopped in front of her, waiting for the light to turn green. Pria had enough time to look at the sole passenger. A beautiful woman in her late twenties, staring out the window. Their eyes met for a moment, then the woman looked down at Pria's legs.

Is that a look of jealousy on her face? I should be envious of her, she's gorgeous and George is her driver. Maybe because she's in a wheelchair? I wish I looked like her. Wish I looked like anyone else, just not like me.

The light changed and the van drove off. Pria decided a mere glimpse of George wouldn't do. There had to be a way to find him, and perhaps if she could work up the courage, talk to him. She wondered if he still lived with his mother. Likely. Next week, Pria would investigate. She couldn't do it tomorrow. Wednesdays were for something else. Changing her schedule could be disastrous for her.

Opening her purse, she looked inside, noting the contents. Wallet. Tweezers. No notebook. No pen. She'd memorize the phone number of the pool by putting it to music. Using her special song, she hummed: 5—5—5—2—1—3—4, 5—5—5—2—1—3—4, 5—5—5—2—1—3—4. The third time through, the phone number implanted itself in her brain.

Weary of waiting for the next bus, Pria decided to walk in the direction of her apartment. It was at least four miles back to where she lived, but one of Pria's goals was to start walking more. On a daily basis. This was the first goal she ever created that didn't have a day attached to it. Pria wasn't sure if it was a good or bad idea.

The Plucker

To pass the time during her journey home Pria thought back on the one time she'd interacted with George. It wasn't a very long interaction, but its memory stayed with her for years. It was the spark that kept her hope of a friendship with George alive.

She saw George sitting under a tree on the far edge of the playground. It was the first day of second grade. This was the third year she was lucky enough to be in the same classroom as him. Pria found out later that Mrs. Franks, her kindergarten teacher, intervened and asked the registrar to always put George and Pria in the same classroom.

She thought about him all summer and planned a way to get his attention. Pria discovered George liked to collect things, but wasn't sure what. He didn't have any other interests as far as she knew. If she started collecting something maybe he would be curious and ask her about it.

Pria's only collection was a tin box filled with the magic strings that grew out of her forearm. She hadn't dared to share them with anyone. Maybe George would understand. She transferred them into a little baggie that day and stuffed them in her coat pocket, unsure she would have the courage to show George. She kept circling closer and closer to the tree where he sat. Settling on the grass a foot away from George, she pulled the bag out of her pocket, weighing it in her small hand. Without looking at him she tossed the baggie on the ground in front of him and held her breath.

George met Pria's eyes for a moment. Then he picked up the baggie, shaking it to separate the strings. Gazing at the contents for a few seconds, he tossed it back to Pria. No words passed between them, but a connection had been made. At least in Pria's mind.

The sound of a baseball game brought Pria back to the present. She stopped to watch the Little League game for a few minutes. Her brows began to tingle. Time to come up with a plan or she'd succumb to uncontrollable plucking.

She would join the Blue Lake Community Pool.

Pria hadn't been swimming for a long time, unsure of her skill, embarrassed by her skinny body. But if her plan to run into George were to have a chance of working, she had no choice. Joining the community pool would be a way to run into him without seeming like a stalker.

She wondered if she was a stalker. If so, it wasn't for an evil or twisted reason; Pria simply wanted to connect with her childhood crush. But for what? Companionship? Love?

Pria's self-imposed solitude became her invisible prison.

The Plucker

The following Tuesday, Pria woke up nervous about her plan. She remembered she didn't own a swimsuit, and her body shyness threatened to sabotage her chance of running into George.

Pria went through her morning ritual then sat at her kitchen table with a cup of chai. Her small hands wrapped around the green mug, comforting her while she thought about what she needed to do next.

She hadn't worn a bathing suit in years. The last time was when she was a small girl. Her parents wanted her to take swimming lessons. They weren't swimmers but thought it would be a good idea for her since it seemed all children in America knew how to swim.

After the first lesson, Pria begged her mother not to make her return. She hated the staring and told her mother she didn't like the water. Sunita insisted she return and learn to swim. It was an agonizing six weeks for Pria.

Every week after Pria's swimming lesson a light bulb blew out in her home. Never again did her mother insist that Pria do something she didn't want to. Sunita tamped down the fear that Pria might be the cause and stored it in a small compartment in her brain marked 'Don't think about it.'

Pria put a white long-sleeved cover-up in her purse, knowing she would wear it on top of her swimsuit. Not wanting to reveal the strings on her forearm proved more important than worrying about her body. The mall was on the way to the community center, so Pria picked up a swimsuit there.

"Did you want to sign up for swimming lessons, young lady?" The elderly man at the front desk stopped inputting Pria's information into the computer, waiting for an answer.

"No…no, I think I still remember how to swim. I'm only interested in using the therapy pool."

"Do you have an injury? If so, we need to know so we can inform the lifeguards."

"I'm fine, really, I'm fine. I want to swim in the therapy pool because it isn't as deep and is much warmer. I don't like cold water." Pria shivered as she said this to emphasize her point.

Registration completed, Pria entered the women's locker room and froze. It was filled with naked women. Unashamed, laughing women. She looked down at her scrawny body, comparing it to the range of sizes on full display in front of her. None of the women seemed aware of their imperfect bodies.

Pria reached under the back of her hair, twirling a single strand. Increasing the tension, she yanked out her stress. Breathing deep, lowering her eyes, she looked for her locker. It was in the corner, halfway open. Inside, an old moldy towel.

The Plucker

Taking her pre-swim shower, Pria thought about George.

He's lonely like me. Will he think I'm weird when I 'run into' him? What if he doesn't remember me? Maybe this is a stupid idea.

Pria walked through the locker room hiding her wet, now sheer shirt from the other women. The entrance to the pool was marked on the furthest door. The beginning of a new life or one of shame?

There appeared to be a therapy session going on. One side of the pool was roped off. An instructor was helping a young woman with floating. Pria was mesmerized by the peace on the woman's lovely face. She had her eyes closed, her lips parted into a relaxed smile. It was the woman from the van.

Pria watched as the woman floated, lost in the warm embrace of each drop of water. Millions holding her mangled body, enfolded in their balminess, allowing her to remember euphoria. Her true self found in the pool. Tranquility.

Rather than get into the water, Pria decided to watch the session, hoping to learn something. She hadn't been in a pool since childhood. Pria slid onto the poolside bench near the woman and her therapist, eavesdropping.

She belongs in the water, so serene, so beautiful, like a mermaid.

Once the young woman was hoisted out of the pool, Pria followed her to the locker room. She watched, fascinated by the woman's self-sufficiency. She had no helper but was able to shower and change her clothes. She never smiled, yet seemed content.

Pria left the building, sitting on a bench outside, waiting for the young woman to roll out in her wheelchair. Moments later, the woman appeared. She moved herself toward the sidewalk, set the brake on her wheelchair, and waited for her ride.

Pria felt a tingle in her left hand—the excitement and stress of the imminent meeting made her feel anxious. The van pulled up to the sidewalk. Pria stood, smoothing down her clothes, then walked toward her new life, a stiff smile plastered on her face. The doors opened, and she looked up into the face of an old man.

It wasn't George.

Chapter Four

Pria entered her apartment determined to find George. She didn't have enough money to hire a private detective. She suspected that only happened on television. Starting with the phone book, she looked him up. No luck. Then she thought to try his mother, but couldn't remember her first name. She had no choice. She called her own mother.

"Hello, Mother, this is Pria."

"What do you mean, this is Pria? I know your voice. I'm your mother. What is it? You never call on a Tuesday. Are you hurt? Do you want to move home? We still have a room for you. I knew you'd come back some day…"

Pria could hear her father in the background asking who was calling. He wanted his tea and told her to hang up, they didn't need to buy anything.

"Ranjeet, hold on, it is not a salesperson, it's your daughter. She is calling and I'm worried. She never calls on a Tuesday."

This familiar interchange, although differently worded this time, always happened when she called. Sometimes her parents went on for a few minutes before getting back to her. Today, her mother's worry cut short their conversation.

"Pria, now your father is worried. You know it is bad for him to worry."

"Mother, please let me speak."

Silence on the other end of the line. Worried she'd offended her sensitive mother, Pria felt the urge to pluck something.

"I want to ask you one simple question. That's all. I'm fine, and I'm not moving home."

"Well, then, what is it?"

"Do you remember the name of George's mother?"

"Who? Who is George?"

"He lived in the house four doors down from us. It was the little brown house with black shutters."

"Oh, the strange, heavy child."

"Yes, that's him. What is his mother's first name?"

More silence, then Sunita yelled to Ranjeet in the kitchen.

The Plucker

"What is the name of that woman who lived in the old brown house in our old neighborhood, the one that should have been torn down?"

Pria couldn't hear her father's mumbled answer. She waited for her mother.

"It's a strange name. Something like Lilyath, or Lilya. Let me think…"

Pria's cuticles called to her, but it was the wrong day.

"Lilith! Yes, that is her name."

"Thank you. I have to go now. I have lots to do."

"Wait, Pria, will you visit soon? You haven't been home in weeks. I want to make a special dinner for you. I know you only eat garbage. I could make a nice curry for you."

"I'll let you know, I've been busy, but yes, I'll visit."

Tuesday's agenda changed from trying something new to finding George. Before she made any other plans, Pria opened her hope chest at the foot of her bed. She used to call it a blanket chest but learned early on that girls filled these boxes with items for their future homes. A quaint American custom.

Under her winter blankets were a pile of school photos. Kindergarten through fourth grade, she was in the same class as George. She'd always been tiny, the photographer asking her to stand in the front. George stood behind her, oblivious to her interest. He wasn't smiling.

Neither was she.

Sitting on the bus the following Tuesday, Pria placed herself in a good position to notice the other riders. There were half a dozen misfits sizing each other up with sidelong glances. Heads inclined toward snippets of conversation. She noticed her own head leaning in their direction.

She heard a couple discussing their new apartment, distracting her from her thoughts. An elderly man whispered something to an imaginary seat partner. A baby girl squealed and giggled as her mother tickled her and told her she loved her. Pria pulled her head back and began to plan.

Preparing herself for her visit to George's mother, Pria wondered how much she should disclose and whether she should lie.

Little white lies were harmless. She wouldn't tell someone their outfit looked awful. Telling a white lie was kinder than the alternative. Does a person really want to tell their cousin her baby is ugly? *I've led my life being nice. Never wanting to hurt feelings. So far it's worked for*

The Plucker

me. At a friend's house for dinner, would I ever say the roast is drier than the desert, or that I don't like eggplant? Dare I tell my coworker her husband is anything other than perfect? This way of thinking had never failed her. No reason to change today.

And yet that was her dilemma. What if telling a white lie endangered others, yet helped her to maintain her own delusion? If she told George's mother he didn't really know her, had never spoken to her, she'd slam the door on her.

Pria pressed the button for her stop, getting off a few blocks from her destination. She needed the extra time to work up her courage. Plus she wanted to see her former neighborhood. First she walked past her old house. The new owners had painted it white.

White. Such a boring color.

The garden looked better than when she and her family lived there. No one in her family cared about gardening.

She stood in front of the house for several minutes, remembering her childhood. Her face reflected her memories. Smile. Frown. Smile. Anger. The front door opened, startling her. Pria moved on, not wanting to talk to anyone. Wiping a tear from her cheek, she put her head down and kept walking.

George's house. The last time Pria was in this neighborhood she was in elementary school. Yet

George's place appeared unchanged. There were houses on both sides of his home, but his house looked lonely. Grass overgrown, roof in need of repair, mailbox leaning over. Nothing changed.

This would not be the day she talked to George's mother. She couldn't bring herself to go to the door and knock. Her body began to shake and her heart raced. Nausea set in. It was enough to see the house. She'd try again next Tuesday.

Pria boarded the bus disappointed in her lack of courage. She didn't know Lilith, but had heard rumors she was odd and mean. Confronting someone like that would be difficult to do. Watching the blocks speed by, Pria knew she'd never return if she didn't talk to George's mother today.

She got off a mile from Lilith's house. Finding a bench to sit on, Pria waited until she felt ready.

Lilith opened the door one quarter of an inch, peering out with one squinting blue cataract-ridden eye.

"Go away, I don't want anything!"

She slammed the door without waiting for a reply from Pria, turning the deadbolt.

Now what?

The Plucker

She grabbed a strand of hair from the back of her head and started twisting it around her finger, deciding whether to give up on talking to Lilith. Or could she recover her courage enough to knock again? The strand of hair was wound on her finger next to the roots of her scalp. She was ready to yank when she heard the deadbolt again.

"Why are you still my porch? Go away! I'll call the police if you don't go away!"

"Wait, wait! You know me, but you probably don't recognize me. I lived down the street from you when I was a little girl."

Lilith opened the door a little wider, looking Pria up and down several times. A glimmer of recognition showed on her face. Her perpetually sour visage changed to suspicion.

"Why are you here? You're a member of that Indian family. Never could understand why you people moved here. What could you possibly want from me? No one ever wants anything from me."

"Well, Mrs...."

"Just call me Lilith. I don't want to be reminded of my husband."

"Well, Lilith, I used to be a friend of your son George."

"Him? He never had any friends, what are you talking about? That's his problem—he's a freak. His only friends were dolls. Now he's with some weird robot. Maybe he thought building a robot would replace the stupid action figures I threw away."

"A robot? Well...I want to get in touch with him. Do you happen to know where he's living now? I thought it would be fun to catch up after all these years, since we were good friends and all."

Previous guilt about her white lie was starting to bother her, but she kept on hoping Lilith would disclose George's location.

"Well, you won't be able to visit him. Sorry, little girl or young woman, whatever you are now. If you're a *friend* of George's you must be in your twenties. He's locked away with all the other loonies."

Lilith looked very pleased with herself when she divulged this information. She almost, but not quite, cracked her face into a small, sly smile. Her cataract-veiled eyes bored into Pria's face, challenging her with this information.

Locked away?

Pria couldn't hide her shock at this statement, wondering if this was some sick joke on the part of George's mother. She'd heard Lilith was strange and cruel, but she couldn't let herself believe a mother would lock her son away.

"Do you mean he's sick?"

The Plucker

Yes, you could say he's sick. He's been nothing but trouble since he was born. He takes after his father, that creep. George is just as crazy, and I felt it was my duty as his mother to get him help." Lilith said this with sincerity only she could believe.

"Where is he locked up, please? I'd still like to visit him if that's possible. I know those places have visiting days," Pria said, trying to keep the desperation out of her voice.

Lilith continued to stare at Pria, trying to figure out what to say next. Pria stared back with what she hoped was confidence. Anyone walking by would think they were two people enjoying a pleasant conversation until they observed the faces on both sides. No one blinked for several seconds. Then Pria looked down at her shoes, sensing defeat, until a new thought came to her.

"Well, maybe I can ask your husband. Would he be willing to talk to me?"

"Sure, if you want to go to a séance or something. That ass is dead."

"Oh, I'm so sorry, I didn't know. I didn't mean to bring up something so sad and horrible."

"Oh, you're quite a stupid girl, aren't you? He died when George was a little boy. One day he just… just… disappeared. Haven't seen him since." Lilith challenged Pria with her eyes, daring her to ask what happened.

"Then please let me plead with you. I would really like to see George. I won't ever bother you again; you'll never have to look at my face. Just let me know where he is and I'll leave you in peace."

Pria felt a pressure in her head, that awful pressure she sometimes couldn't control. Her bad self, clawing to escape.

Lilith turned to look behind her, then back at Pria. It sounded like something broke in the kitchen. Lilith didn't have any pets, and no one lived with her, so she wondered what happened but didn't dare leave this person on her doorstep unattended.

"Fine, just leave me alone. George is at the county hospital. Don't ever come back here again."

"Thank you. Do you have a message for George?" Pria felt calmer.

"As if," Lilith sneered, slamming the door.

Entering the kitchen, Lilith was shocked to see the exploded overhead light, the glittering shards of white glass sprinkled on her kitchen floor, a light dusting of snow on this hot summer day. She felt herself shiver, somehow knowing Pria caused this.

Damn freaky Indian girl. George deserves her.

Pria felt like skipping as she walked down the steps of George's old home. Now that she had his location she could make some plans. Fleetingly she wondered if anything bad happened inside his house, knowing she'd lost control of herself for a few moments. There was no way to know; she was never going back to that awful woman and her dilapidated house. Whatever happened, she probably deserved.

A mental hospital? George's mother should be there, not him! Why didn't he refuse? How did she do it?

Dark skies and threatening rain contrasted with Pria's ebullient mood. She was closer to finding George.

Chapter Five

Wednesday. Oh, Wednesday, the best plucking day of all. Pria went to the park to pluck pigeons. The covetous birds loved the crumbs of cornbread she used to lure them. Closer, they ventured, greedily pecking at the morsels of golden goodness.

Chubby Chloe—she named each bird—remained her favorite. That bird edged its way to the front of the flock, grabbing more cornbread than any of the others. Pria wished she could be so forward. Instead, she meekly observed the birds filling their stomachs. Their cooing reminded her of the birds that nested outside her old house. The neighborhood she lived in as a child. The place George lived.

Her parents left the neighborhood when Pria moved out. Her mother told her the house felt empty without her, so they moved into a smaller house, settling into their new life. Sunita maintained a room for Pria, although resigned to her daughter's independence.

Pria only plucked two feathers from each plump bird. It was perfect. Once she'd acquired twenty-one feathers, she stopped. Seven goes into twenty-one three times. She decided to name the number twenty-one *pigeon*, in honor of her favorite day. Pria didn't realize it was strange she insisted on using the term *pigeon* instead of the actual number.

This unusual part of her lexicon began after her first day of gathering feathers from her friends. It seemed right to honor the sacrifice the pigeons made. Not wanting to be greedy, two feathers per bird seemed enough. After ten birds, she had twenty plumes, but then Chubby Chloe appeared for the first time, sidling up to Pria, begging for food and attention. Chloe received the honor of having only one feather plucked that day.

From that day forward, twenty-one became the perfect number to Pria.

The cornbread Pria fed to the birds was baked from her own recipe, perfected after making it hundreds of times. Pria's mother tried to teach her to make curries and naan, but she preferred casseroles and cornbread. And hamburgers. Americans ate hamburgers. Peanut butter and jelly, the only American food she ate growing up, the lure of all things not of her culture drew her away from her family's traditions.

Betty Crocker's Cookbook became her guide to cooking all things American. Pria loved the organization of the three-ring binder of recipes, complete with categories including meat, dessert, and salads. The instructions were easy and the photos let her know if she was on the right track. It was the most perused book on her tiny bookshelf.

Once the cornbread was baked, Pria would move on to preparing casseroles for her dinners. Her favorite, tuna casserole, she ate at least once a week. The crumbled potato chips on the surface of the molten cheese felt comforting to her palate. When the cheese burned her mouth, she played with the blisters and loose skin with her tongue.

Crumbling the golden cornbread, Pria tossed the morsels to her avian friends. They cooed in appreciation in the direction of their benefactor. Pigeons were intelligent, contrary to popular belief; they understood having their feathers plucked was the price of their free meal. Pria hoped they also understood the honor involved. She felt they did.

The Plucker

The third time Pria sat on the park bench with her bag of crumbs, the wily birds gathered at her feet, waiting with an abundance of patience to pay for their meal. No jostling, their natural behavior overridden by a desire for a free feast. Cooing almost in unison, a feast song to accompany the banquet.

Her small friends liked it when she hummed. It wasn't a particular song, just a riff of tones they and she found soothing. Several visits in, Pria understood the tune contained the notes she strummed on her guitar. E, B, G, D, A, E. Her soothing notes now pleased her pigeons.

The pigeons and Pria were a tight-knit group, meeting once a week for the last three years. They accepted her as she was. She adored them. The stable group was a comfort to her, a source of predictable company. For them, an expected bounty of sustenance. No need for a change until today.

A new pigeon joined the hungry group, staying on the edge. It looked at Pria as if asking permission to join. Before deciding, Pria turned to Chubby Chloe to observe whether she knew this bird. Chloe tilted her head in understanding, nodding in the affirmative. Delighted, Pria cooed to the new member of her family, naming the bird George.

George became part of the gang. He ate more than any of the other pigeons, winning the title of Chubby from Chloe. Pria chose not to pluck George; it seemed wrong to her. The human George might be offended.

Pria leaned back on the park bench feeling the glow of satisfaction. Her friends were gathered around her, the sun was shining, and she was exactly where she wanted to be. Today she would stay longer. Nothing else needed to be done.

While the pigeons were busily gobbling up the golden goodness, Pria decided to look around at the other people in the park. An old couple seated two benches down was chatting, children played across the way kicking a ball, but no one seemed to be as happy as she was.

She leaned back, closing her eyes for a few minutes. Not a nap. An opportunity for her to reflect. To quiet her busy mind. To absorb the sun's warmth. It was a time to remember.

Before she started school, Pria adored her mother and tolerated her father. He didn't pay attention to her. Not from lack of love—she was a girl, her mother's territory. When prompted, he'd pat Pria on the top of her head and bestow a kiss on her cheek.

The Plucker

Every morning her mother sang as she prepared breakfast, stopping to pick up her delicate child and swing her around while dancing. She fed Pria tiny morsels of love, the tasty bits of the meal. During the day, Pria followed her mother like a duckling, never losing sight of her. Trying to touch her mother as often as she could. At first crawling, then later with unsure drunken toddler steps, always moving toward the center of her universe. The sunshine in her world. The time to move away would come later.

If the day was sunny, they'd eat their lunch in their backyard. Their favorite spot under the apple tree. Pria liked to watch the clouds, finding animal shapes. The next-door neighbor heard a squeaky little voice yell, 'Squirrel, bunny, turtle!' Then came laughter. Giggling, she loved it when Sunita mimicked animal sounds, trying to match the animal Pria saw with the sound they made. Turtle always stumped Sunita.

Sunita's brow was not yet furrowed, her smile the most prominent feature of her face. Her only child, Pria, her gift from the gods. She couldn't resist pinching her soft cheeks and nuzzling the black fuzz on top of her perfect round head. She watched the fuzz become strong black hair falling straight down from the crown of Pria's head as her daughter grew.

Pria's dark eyes observed everything her mother did. Smiled while watching her mother wrap her sari around her body. Fascinated by the jangling bracelets on her mother's round arms. Pria grabbed a bracelet, trying to eat it. Sunita turned and laughed at her silly child. No need for anyone to enter their perfect world. This was all they needed: each other.

One day her father suggested Sunita take Pria to the park. He wanted his daughter to meet other children. Sunita resisted, not wanting to let the world in. The first furrow began to etch itself on her brow. Change was coming. Her stomach began to ache in anticipation.

After weeks of urging, Sunita and Pria went outside, walking to the nearby playground. Pria's world grew from her safe house and yard to an unknown realm. She pointed toward the play structure surprised by what was in front of her; she'd never seen swings or a slide.

Pria pulled away from Sunita, running with undisguised glee. Excited to jump on the shiny metal things in front of her. Not noticing the other children yet, single-minded in her goal to reach the structures. She didn't see the other mothers staring at her, but her own mother did.

She climbed onto a swing, not sure what to do next. Looking at her mother, Pria waited. Sunita began to push her daughter with a gentle nudge, not wanting her to fall off. Pria kept saying, "More, Mommy!" So

Sunita increased the speed. Pria was soaring and she loved it.

Finished flying, Pria looked around, deciding where to explore. Next destination: the slide. Pria figured out how to use it by watching the other children. She'd noticed them while soaring on the swing. They were a squirming pale mass of laughter and running.

At the top of the slide she paused to make sure her mother saw her. Then she held her breath and slid down the long, shiny piece of metal, gathering speed. She bounced at the bottom and took a deep breath. Silence for a few moments. Then a loud laugh.

"Again, Mommy, again!"

A little boy waited in front of her for his turn. He looked back at her and frowned. Reaching for her arm, he asked, "Does the brown wipe off?"

Confused, Pria stared back at the boy. She didn't know how to answer such a bizarre question. In her four-year-old mind, there was no reason for him to ask her such a thing. She ran her own hand along her arm. Turning her palm upwards, she showed it to the boy.

"No, it stays brown."

On the way home she asked Sunita about the boy's question. Another furrow began to form on Sunita's brow. She wasn't sure what to say to her precious daughter. This was the beginning of the awful change she'd feared.

Hearing loud cooing, Pria looked down to find all her pigeon friends staring at her. Still hungry, asking for more. She opened her purse and pulled out her emergency bag of cornbread. Sometimes her friends needed more. Or they knew they could get more when she stayed longer. She sprinkled the crumbs and watched her friends eating in companionable silence.

She laughed, noticing George was in the center of the pigeons grabbing as many morsels of cornbread as he could. She marveled at how fast he could eat. The other pigeons didn't seem to mind, they moved over a little and let George go for it.

Time to leave, but she wasn't ready. Her precious time with her pigeon friends had flown by. She decided to linger even longer and enjoy the day and the company of Chloe, George, and the others.

"George, come here, my pretty bird."

All the pigeons looked up at Pria, but only George stepped forward, rubbing his beak against her leg then looking into her brown eyes with beady orange ones. She stroked his feathers, humming and smiling.

The Plucker

"What should I do with all the feathers I've collected, George?" She paused, expecting an answer. He continued to stare into her eyes, his way of replying.

"I could make a cape of feathers! I wonder how difficult that is? Maybe I should stop at the library and find out. I haven't been there for ages, George."

George rejoined the other pigeons, no longer interested in Pria or her question. They left en masse, looking for another benefactor. Pria fought the urge to feel sad. She'd see them again next week.

Walking home from the park, Pria thought about George—the human—and his new life in an institution. She felt guilty about her pleasant visit with her pigeon friends, assuming George was miserable now.

He is miserable, isn't he? How could he be otherwise?

Pria's only point of reference for life in a mental institution was from books and movies. She thought everyone in those hospitals were unhappy. Could there be another experience there? George never needed the company of others, so would living in that place make any difference to him?

Approaching her apartment door, she shook her head. Of course he was miserable. If she didn't help him, no one would. It was time to brainstorm ideas. There must be a way for her to make a difference in his life.

Chapter Six

Thursday, Friday, and Saturday were workdays for her. The pickle factory. Her job was quality assurance, though she never called it QA. As the thousands of pickles flew past on the conveyor belt, Pria was paid, yes, paid by the factory, to pluck bad pickles and toss them into a bin behind her. She told herself she relished her job, giggling at her pun.

Watching the bumpy pickles whiz past her on their way to the waiting jars mesmerized her. Her sharp eyes spotted the misfits, the castoffs, the cousins of Pria. Pausing for a moment to run her fingers over the bumps, she tossed the rejects over her shoulder.

If she missed the bin, she mentally added shame points to herself. Once Pria reached five points, she took a break, rushing to the bathroom. Secure in a stall, she pulled one hair for each point from the lower back of her scalp. Saving these for later, she returned to the conveyor belt.

Feeling refreshed, Pria continued with her important task of keeping ugly pickles from the hungry public. Pride. She felt pride in her task. And satisfaction in her ability to spot the unwanted vegetables. Not everyone could do her job. Never bored or tired, she plucked until her shift ended.

She wished George could witness how proficiently she performed her job. This pride, a rare occurrence for Pria, became the focal point of her thoughts. George would be impressed. Impressed enough to love her. Perhaps. Or at least like her.

Her parents wondered why Pria had chosen this job. She was smart, but hated school. After high school she moved out, living on her graduation money until she found this perfect job. The description enticing, the work satisfying. What more could she want? Her obsession was now a source of income.

During orientation, Pria's excitement about her new job rose as she toured the building. The company gave her a personal locker, a special apron, and her own spot on the conveyor belt. Only Pria would be in charge of quality assurance during her shift. That was good. She preferred to work alone.

The rest of the staff posed a problem for her. They wanted to chat while working, and during breaks. Pria didn't know how to chat, but she learned to mimic the speech patterns and topics of her co-workers. She convinced herself she fit in at last. The kinder ones let her believe it.

The bell for quitting time brought Pria back from her head. Standing in front of her small locker she shed her work facade. Apron, hairnet, gloves, and frozen smile. All tucked into her locker until next Thursday. She patted the outside of the rusty locker three times then turned to walk out to the city bus.

At home, eating her small meal of cornbread and tuna casserole, Pria thought about the design to use for a bracelet. She'd pulled enough shame-points hair to weave one. Or perhaps she would make a necklace. No. Not enough shame yet. A shame bracelet would do for now. A reminder of her failure to be perfect at her job. Her life.

Clearing away her chipped green plate, she fetched her baggie of long black hair. Her mother had taught her to braid her thick hair as a child, so making a bracelet would be easy. Taking three strands, she wove them together. She repeated the process until she had enough. Pria gathered the *pigeon* braids, tying them together on one end.

She used the macramé skills she'd been taught during her stint in therapy as a child. Reaching the end of the bracelet, Pria added a small silver bell. Each time it tinkled she would be reminded of her failure. Of her lack of perfection.

The delicate bracelet looked good against Pria's caramel skin. There was enough hair left to make another one, pleasing her. And confusing her. If there was more hair, she'd failed too often. She made the second bracelet and admired how it adorned her other wrist. She shook both wrists, closed her eyes, and listened.

Should I wear my bracelets every day or only on special occasions? No, what special occasions? There aren't any. Every day is best. I need to be reminded daily of my need to improve.

The phone rang, making Pria jump. The only person who called her was her mother. The phone rang seven times then went to voicemail, which was nearing capacity. She needed to read the instructions for deleting messages on Sunday. Her quick fix for today: turn off the ringtone.

Pria's after-dinner walk took her to the park several blocks away. There was a path she favored because it wound around a small lake. Blue Lake. Misnamed because the lake was filled with milfoil and duck droppings. But still, she loved it there. Everyone seemed intent on finishing the lake's loop without stopping.

Before starting her way around the lake Pria enjoyed watching the intent exercisers, marveling at their tenacity. Her nightly walks were now a routine, but she still had to force herself out the door. Easier to stay home, drink tea, and think about the upcoming day. Each evening she was glad she made herself go outside.

There seemed to be a lot of cyclists on the trail this evening, which worried her. She never felt fast enough on the trail when the bicycles came screaming up from behind. Pria attempted to find an opening on the path by observing how often a group of cyclists passed by. It was time to step onto the trail and begin her walk.

No one noticed the small brown woman with long black hair scurrying to the safety of the walking path. The cyclists didn't yield to the pedestrians. Pria didn't want to get knocked over, so she found her spot on the path, staying to the far edge, and felt safe. She began her stroll around the lake.

Tonight she noticed geese lingering by the side of the water. Geese were trouble. She felt a familiar childhood fear of those mean-spirited birds. A memory of being chased by a loud gaggle, of being rescued by her father. Then a branch had fallen off a tree, crushing some of the geese. The shocked look on her father's face as he looked from his little girl to the mass of bloody birds under the branch was not easily forgotten.

Nearing the halfway point of her circuit around the lake she heard footsteps behind her. Turning, Pria saw the deep-breathing woman from the bus. The blonde. The woman seemed intent on passing Pria, pumping her arms, head down, swiveling her hips to gain speed.

Pria respected her enthusiasm and energy, knowing she would be too embarrassed to exercise in such an attention-grabbing manner. She tried for a few steps and felt the slow burn of a blush. Her gentler way of walking, arms at her side, taking short steps, suited her.

Quiet surrounded her again while Pria enjoyed the soft tinkling of her shame bracelets. Soothing her. The rest of her time at the lake she spent thinking about nothing. The bells produced a meditative state.

Entering her silent apartment, Pria greeted her fireplace shrine with a nod of her head. The guitar, vase, and jar kept her company, protection from loneliness lurking outside her door. Her welcoming home, drawing her in.

She turned on her small color television with a built-in DVD player, a luxury she'd saved a year to buy. Inserting one of her favorite movies, Pria settled in with a cup of chai, ready to leave reality, immersing herself into the fantasy of Hollywood.

The love story took place between a blind man and a beautiful woman, the woman always wary of the intentions of men. None were able to see past her looks. The blind man met her, but unable to see her, fell in love with her essence. The real woman. Pria adored this movie, watching it every week. She'd memorized the dialogue, mouthing the words with the actors as they spoke.

Her heart swelled with longing as the movie proceeded to its expected climax. The beautiful woman and the blind man in love for all the right reasons. The reasons Pria thought people should have to be in love. At the end of the movie she sat quietly, staring out her window, watching the moon. She saw the same face in the moon she always did. Full moons were her favorite because she would see his entire face. His chubby, round, solemn face. George.

Apart from the movies, romance was never a part of her existence; this was as close as she'd managed to love. The fictional characters lived the life she wanted, loving the way she dreamed was perfect. The life she might have someday with George.

An accustomed burning rose on her cheeks, a blush she could never control. Glad for once her skin wasn't princess white, both hands cupped her cheeks, feeling the warmth of her desire.

She played the 'what if' game with herself. What if she found George? What if he didn't recognize her? What if he did? What if they had a life together? What if her obsession with finding him was wrong?

The last question disturbed her. Why was she so determined to find a childhood friend who never noticed her? Her loneliness. Despair filled her heart, threatening to break it. Her hands came together of their own volition, plucking at her cuticles in an attempt to distract her from her pain.

A familiar heat burned the back of her head, causing her to tremble. She knew what was next and tried to control it, but it was beyond her now. Letting go, it would happen, she had no choice. Or she thought she didn't.

Pria put her hands over her ears so she wouldn't hear the light bulbs breaking in her kitchen. A few moments later she stood up, resigned to an evening of sweeping up glittering glass fragments of isolation. Anger replaced loneliness, the afterglow of watching the movie gone.

Pria lay in bed thinking about the broken light bulbs. The geese when she was a child. The broken window on the bus. Was she a freak? She'd never understood her ability to break things, never figured out how to control it.

Her earliest memory of this strange power was as a child—the horrid six weeks of swim lessons and the weekly exploding of a light bulb in her home. The fear in her mother's eyes.

The Plucker

Pria didn't made things break or explode on purpose, but it seemed to happen whenever she was frustrated, angry, or afraid. Though not able to control this phenomenon, she knew when it was about to happen. Her head heated up, her body tensed, then something bad happened. After the event she would feel release, a calming sensation, a moment of peace. Sometimes guilt.

The next time Pria remembered this happening was during the geese incident. Her father rescued her, yet she couldn't stop being afraid of the noise of the snapping beaks, of the mass of geese running toward her.

Her head felt hot, then suddenly she heard the cracking of an overhead tree branch. It came down and destroyed her enemies, making her feel both relieved and sad.

After that incident her father looked at her the same way her mother did. His widened eyes filled with wonder, fear, and denial. They walked home in silence. This was unusual.

Her father, Ranjeet, wouldn't hold her hand; he kept his hands in the pockets of his slacks, pretending to be cold, never glancing back to see if she was keeping up with him. He hunched his thin shoulders, walking briskly toward the safety of his waiting newspaper. He needed to escape. She could feel that need radiating from him.

Pria refused to think about her strange power any longer. She needed to sleep, to be refreshed for the next day. She wished, not for the first time, to be free of this freaky phenomenon, hoping the act of ignoring it would make it go away. No good could come of it. She remained convinced it would eventually harm someone she loved.

Her solution: to stop feeling emotions. If fear, anger, or frustration triggered this, she would learn to maintain an even keel. To enter a meditative state where nothing bothered her. She tinkled the bells on her bracelets as a reminder of that peaceful state.

Turning over in bed, she pulled her covers closer, snuggling in for a deep, dreamless sleep. Tomorrow was Sunday. Her day of rest came every other week.

Chapter Seven

Pria jumped out of bed. Sunday! She hurried to the kitchen to turn on her tea kettle. The sun was shining outside, filtering pink light through her curtains, coloring everything inside with a rosy glow. It was going to be a good day.

Humming, she prepared the items needed. They were stored in her linen closet, in a wooden box, a gift from her mother. The intricate carvings on the outside reminded her of the culture she loathed. The shame of being different had never left her. Using the box kept her vigilant against falling into the trap of her ethnicity.

On Pria's non-plucking Sundays, she rested. Eyebrows required this time to grow. Plucked cuticles needed to repair themselves. Her tired brain needed to reset for another busy week of plucking.

Pria never left her apartment on those Sundays. No one would understand her appearance on her day of rest. She needed to be alone to heal her body and refresh her mind. Being alone refilled her after days of depletion, pretending, acting, being not-Pria.

Her black cotton gloves covered hands slathered in lotion. The thick lotion helped her cuticles to heal and prevented her from any errant plucking. Pria covered her face with her gloved hands, breathing in the aroma of vanilla.

Vanilla reminded her of ice cream with her parents. On ice cream days they walked to an ice cream parlor in town, each selecting their favorite flavor. Her father chose chocolate, her mother favored pistachio, Pria remained true to vanilla. Not a boring flavor. A flavor of possibilities, a malleable vessel of taste.

On her face, she wore an old Halloween mask. It served the same purpose as the gloves, preventing her from disturbing her eyebrows. More importantly, it let Pria pretend to be someone else. Her only chance at a new face. She knew it was weird to wear these masks, but felt compelled every other Sunday to do so. She had three to choose from: Wonder Woman, a mermaid, and a princess. Today she hid behind the princess mask. Looking at herself in the mirror, she wished, not for the first time, that this was her real face. This would be her face in a perfect life. Blonde hair, blue eyes, and porcelain skin. Pria hid her brown behind this plastic facade.

I know it's strange, maybe twisted, but I'm not crazy.

The first time Pria put on a mask was Halloween. She was five years old and wore a princess costume. Her parents didn't want her going around begging for candy. In their view that's what all the neighborhood children were all doing, begging. They did not come from a family of beggars.

Pria brought home a flyer from school informing the students they could dress up on Friday. This forced Ranjeet and Sunita's hand—they had to allow their daughter to wear a costume. They didn't want to be ashamed to have the only child without one.

Sunita offered to sew her daughter a beautiful sari to wear to school on Friday. Even at five Pria knew she didn't want to wear something from India. She'd seen a movie about a princess named Cinderella and wanted to be dressed up exactly like her. She convinced her mother to take her to the mall and shop for her outfit.

"Why do you wish to be so difficult? I could sew you a beautiful costume and then we wouldn't have to go to the mall. You would look lovely in a pink sari."

"Mommy, I don't like saris. I don't want to wear one, no one else has one at my school. I don't want to be the only one wearing something strange. Please, Mommy, I know what I want. I want to be a princess."

The remainder of their drive was silent. Sunita was sad her daughter was ashamed of her culture. Amazed that at her young age she'd already learned to see the difference between herself and her classmates. Worried that being ashamed so early in life would affect her later on. Sunita didn't know what to do.

There was an entire section of the store devoted to Halloween costumes. Sunita was surprised at the variety of costumes and obvious popularity of this bizarre holiday. Pria pulled her mother by the arm toward the princess display, excited about how she would look. The round rack jammed full of glittery pink outfits filled Pria with joy and Sunita with dread.

A miniature replica of the gown Cinderella wore to the grand ball became the focus of Pria's attention. She pulled it off the rack, held it up against her body, and looked up at her mother expectantly. Sunita nodded yes and began to move toward the cash registers.

"Mommy, Mommy, wait the costume isn't finished yet."

Turning back to her daughter, Sunita questioned her with a lift of her eyebrows.

"Mommy, I need a mask still, I can't be Cinderella with my own face, everyone would laugh at me. I don't look like Cinderella."

The Plucker

Pria pointed to a shelf displaying dozens of masks, an array of faces piled according to their category. Celebrities, presidents, monsters, and princesses. Her mother walked over to the display and grabbed a princess mask with dark hair and gave it to her daughter.

"No, Mommy! That's the wrong mask."

"But it has the same hair color as you do, Pria. It's perfect for you to wear for Halloween."

"No, Mommy, Cinderella has blonde hair. She has blue eyes. She has white skin. I want to look like Cinderella."

Her mother sighed with resignation, replacing the dark-haired mask on the display. She stepped back and let her daughter choose. Pria chose the mask with the attributes she described to her mother.

Looking around for a mirror, she found one in the next aisle. She pulled the mask over her face then turned and looked at her reflection. Silence. Then she felt a small tear trickling down her face. She was happy. The happiest she'd felt in her young life.

Every Halloween Pria picked a new princess costume until she was too old to trick-or-treat. The last year she went out she was twelve years old. With sadness, she knew she wouldn't be doing it again.

The day after Halloween, Pria stopped at a store after school and purchased three masks marked down for clearance. She put them in a box and hid them in the back of her closet knowing someday she'd have a use for them. They were the same three masks she used now.

To assuage her need to pluck on this non-plucking day, she had a supply of Bubble wrap. Breaking the bubbles produced a similar feeling of release. Pria acknowledged this wasn't a substitute for the rush she felt while plucking, but not doing anything wouldn't do. It was her methadone. It kept her urges tamped down, allowing the hair on her body to rest and heal.

She'd heard a disturbing story on the radio about the company who produced Bubble wrap. A change in the gas within the bubbles would eliminate the delicious popping sound. Not knowing if this was simply a rumor, Pria set aside extra money to acquire a larger supply. Allowing herself to imagine the disastrous effect this new soundless Bubble wrap could have on her wasn't an option.

Noting her dwindling supply of Bubble wrap, Pria planned to head to a packaging store the next day, after she played her guitar. Leaving the apartment today was not possible.

She rotated the stores she shopped in. After going to the same one twelve times in a row, always purchasing Bubble wrap, she saw the clerk give her a strange look. He started to speak, changed his mind, and continued to ring up her purchase.

What does he think about me? Does he wonder what I do with all of this? Maybe I can pretend to own a store. But really, do I care what this stranger thinks of me? Yes, I do. Of course I do. I always will.

Now she carried a map of stores that sold Bubble wrap. With each purchase she marked the date next to the store, her intent to never be at the same retailer more than once a month. The added bonus of her plan was she got to see more of her city.

To keep busy on non-plucking Sundays, Pria baked the cornbread her pigeon friends gobbled up. Baking it on Sunday gave the bread time to get a bit stale. She divided the batch into two. One would be for that week, the rest for the week after. Freezing the second batch only after it attained the correct degree of staleness.

By Wednesday, the day she fed her friends, the golden cornbread had the perfect consistency for crumbling and tossing. Pria smiled, thinking about the pigeons. Her pigeons. Her loyal friends. She missed them but wouldn't change her routine. She couldn't. Visits to her pigeons occurred on Wednesdays. Only Wednesdays.

A cat? Could she get a cat to keep her company the rest of the week? *What would the pigeons think of that? Would a cat destroy my fireplace shrine?*

Pria would discuss a cat with her friends. They were good listeners and wouldn't let their natural dislike of felines color their advice to her.

A dog might be a better choice. I could take the dog on my daily walks! It could protect me from the geese. We could be best friends.

A burning smell from the kitchen alarmed Pria. She'd been daydreaming and not paying attention to the time. Running to the oven, she yanked the door open and shrieked.

"No, not my cornbread! It's ruined."

Tossing the baking pan in the sink, she slid down to the floor and stared at the oven. The malicious oven bent on ruining her Wednesday visit. It hated her. Why else would it burn her cornbread?

A loud pop. Something falling on her head. Sparkly glass snow. She rose and began cleaning up the mess, her kitchen still embedded with the sparkly snow of the last time this occurred. She swept the glistening pile into the corner then nudged it onto the dustpan.

She stared at the broken glass for a bit, thinking how beautiful it looked reflecting the light from the sunset. A fleeting thought. Should she save the sparkling pile in a jar? Pria shook her head and tossed it.

Waving her wrists settled her down as the bells on her bracelets tinkled. Pria knew she'd be up late baking. Her friends would be hungry, they depended on her cornbread. She depended on their company.

Just before midnight, Pria finished baking. After she put the batter in the oven, she sat on a stool staring at the cornbread inside. No mistakes this time, no chance for the golden goodness to burn.

Allowing herself three squares of chocolate, she nibbled the corners, making them last. It was late, but she needed to watch one of her movies. Pria selected a version of *Cinderella* she favored, then pressed play on her remote. She readied herself for a journey to a land of fantasy.

Cinderella dancing with the prince. Love at first sight. In this movie she didn't mind that the prince fell in love with Cinderella because she was beautiful. That was the point of a fairy tale. In a fairy tale everyone lived happily ever after.

She went to bed exhausted but satisfied with the day. Her plans for tomorrow other than the usual Monday ritual were open. It felt liberating not to know what she'd do. A new feeling for Pria. Spontaneity? Almost. She hoped to get to that point someday.

Monday would be whatever she wanted it to be. A new adventure or more of the same. It didn't matter to her as she drifted off to sleep. Tonight she knew what she would dream, her mind still replaying the dance at the ball, her Prince Charming leading her across the dance floor. Her blonde hair flowing luxuriously down her porcelain shoulders.

Chapter Eight

Her days at work were planned so she seemed to fit in. Chatting with co-workers, yet never going out with them.

They pluck so unmercifully at people they laugh at.

She seldom reached for her eyebrows in front of others. Didn't want to be ridiculed. Her brain tried to manage busy fingers, reading a book, turning the pages in a smooth, open-handed motion, ignoring the itchy twitching in her mind. Being someone else to survive.

More whispers today. More heads nodding in her direction. They knew something she did not. Pria sensed a change. Everyone was openly staring at her. Pria concentrated on sorting her pickles, her pride intact. Compelled to continue with her important task of keeping ugly pickles out of jars.

While reaching for her time card at the end of the shift, her supervisor gave her a pink slip. Pria decided not to panic. She plucked it out of his outstretched hand using her public smile. Her co-workers whispered and pointed. Pria ignored them and left the factory. Clutching the pink card, amazed the card was really pink, she tore strips off while walking to the bus stop. Each bright pink strip fluttered behind her, leaving a trail to the factory. A trail backwards to a life she was being forced to give up.

Pria kept one strip of pink to put on her fireplace mantel. It seemed appropriate for her to have a memento of her favorite job amongst her dearest treasures. Her private shrine was growing.

Entering her apartment, Pria carried on. Plucking calendar pages, surveying ways to track the passage of time. Washing a handful of grapes, setting them aside. She would take care of them later. No time to enjoy them now. The room began to spin, her head pounded, her fingers grasping then plucking at her lips.

Rising from the floor, she resolved to find a new job. Pria enjoyed the fruit, plucking one dark orb at a time from its stem, planning her new life. Pulling grapes, the quiet snap relaxing her. The rhythm of her fingers reassuring. Noticing the deep silence following each snap.

The Plucker

The morning paper gifted her with a job. She spotted the tiny ad on the bottom of page *pigeon*. *Pigeon*, Pria's name for twenty-one. Her next job calling to her through smudged ink and newsprint.

"Florist assistant. Thursday through Saturday. No experience required. Must be available immediately," she breathed softly, luring the job closer.

A brief phone conversation led to an in-person interview the next morning. Pria spent the rest of the day choosing her outfit and practicing what she would say. Natural conversation was not her strong point.

As she neared the florist's shop Pria's arms began tingling. Looking around in a panic she noticed an alley. She stepped into the deserted spot for some privacy to relieve her tension. Two plucked strings were enough to calm her down.

"Have you ever done any gardening? Deadheaded flowers? Can you work 6 am to 2 pm? Can you start tomorrow?"

The florist's rapid questions continued for another three minutes. Stopping, he peered at Pria over his half-moon glasses. She nodded yes. Yes to it all. The deal done. For once he wouldn't have to deal with a chatterer.

She was fired after one week. Pria couldn't stop deadheading the faded blooms. She plucked and plucked until all the flowers were bald. Ruining the blooms was not the goal but rather the outcome. Once she started, her fingers wouldn't let her stop.

After each pluck she'd notice another bloom seeming to fade before her eyes, offering itself to her nimble fingers. A job well done is always completed; she had to keep deadheading. Selfish not to pluck a blossom sacrificing itself for her. Pria nodded to each flower as she groomed them.

Her trip home on the bus allowed time for reflection. The loss of her job didn't make her bitter. Frustrated, desolate, but not bitter. Pria's left hand crept up to her eyebrows. Another job was not an issue, the perfect job still eluded her.

Her next endeavor, picking fruit, lasted three days. Stock clerk, seven. Dog walker lasted *pigeon* days. Somehow, the owners found out she'd tied the dogs to a tree in the park. Visiting her pigeon friends instead of exercising their precious pets. The owners called her *irresponsible, weird, useless.*

Refusing to become despondent, Pria used her bus rides to make new resolutions. Her left hand remained motionless in her lap. She spent the time during the bus ride to think about George. As George filled her thoughts, her body relaxed. Her hand crept up to her mouth to confirm her smile.

The bus driver nodded to her as Pria got off at her stop. This always embarrassed her; she preferred to be invisible. Pretending to be normal, she nodded back then hurried down the steps. Resisting the urge to watch the bus pull away, she walked the short distance to her apartment.

A strange set of ideas were trying to escape:

Don't get another job.

Go to school.

Be a nurse's aide.

Work at George's hospital.

Free George.

Pria shook her head, trying to shake the crazy ideas from her brain. It was absurd to think she could rescue George. Strange to consider going back to school. She'd graduated from high school and vowed not to go to college. It didn't interest her, and trying to mix in proved too challenging. But…George.

Scrolling through websites, Pria had a difficult time deciding which school would be the best one for her to attend. Her resources limited, Pria didn't want to ask her parents to help her pay. They would not approve of her choice of a new profession, although they might be happy she was making a change in her life. The pickle factory job shamed them.

Pria couldn't let them know why she wanted this—the sole reason for this change was George. Now that she knew he was locked up at the county hospital she felt compelled to help him. She needed to become a nurse's aide so that she could see him.

Still aghast at the news that his mother had committed him, Pria knew her main goals were to see that George was comfortable and to help him get better. But she also knew that if George couldn't get out she wanted to be near him in any capacity possible.

Pria wasn't patient enough to go back to school to become a full-fledged nurse and found out that nurse's aides spent more time with the patients at this institution. She also realized she would be helping patients other than George, but the thought of feeding, toileting, and keeping patients company didn't deter her from her goal.

Pria searched the catalogs of several community colleges, gathering information on the courses she should be taking. It wouldn't take as long as she thought to get her nurse's aide certification.

Weary of trying to decide which school to attend and anxious to get going with this next phase of her life, Pria used her special number and chose the *pigeon* school on the list. She filled out the online application, confident that they would accept her into their program. Now to wait.

There was just enough in her savings account to pay for tuition if she was careful with her money. Her right hand crept up to her eyebrows, but it was the wrong day. She had to use her willpower to draw her hand back down and prevent it from plucking prematurely.

Walking into the school for the first time Pria noticed the diverse members of her class. Not wanting to be late on her first day, she took a cab to class. It was a small pleasure in her life to have someone drive her. The cost would come out of her entertainment budget, the money she used for buying the movies she watched.

She expected to be surrounded by eighteen or nineteen-year-olds and was pleased to see the students;

it made her feel less alien and more like a part of the group. There were twenty people in the class, an equal mix of males and females. No one seemed to stand out. Each student tried to look busy thumbing through their textbooks while stealing glances at one another.

Pria sat in the last row as far from the nearest student as possible. She wanted to be able to concentrate and needed privacy in case the urge to pluck overwhelmed her during the lesson. She placed her plaid tote bag on the floor, pulling out her brand-new shiny textbook. Pria placed it on her desk. She didn't spend time looking over her classmates, she was too busy trying to get her mind ready for learning.

Ten minutes before class started, Pria started to feel anxious again. Not wanting to reveal her uniqueness, she clasped her hands together tighter, resisting the overwhelming urge to pluck something. After a few more seconds she could no longer stand it and stood up, walking out of the classroom. She made sure there was no one else in the restroom, then she pulled up the sleeve on her left arm.

Just one. Just one…if I pluck just one, that'll get me through the class.

Pria took her tweezers out of her pocket, hovering over the blue thread nearest her elbow, took a deep breath, and pulled. She shivered with delight. Now she should be able to get through the class and concentrate.

The Plucker

The blue thread went into a special container she carried around with her for these types of emergencies. When she returned to her apartment later that evening, Pria would place the precious blue thread in the vase.

The door to the women's bathroom opened, startling Pria. Not knowing if she should stay in the stall or try to escape once the other person was busy, she began to panic. It shouldn't matter to her if someone else saw her in there, they didn't know what she was doing in the stall. She decided to flush the toilet to create a distraction, then strode out with confidence. The other person was already behind another stall door. Pria relaxed and returned to class.

Pria opened the door to the classroom just as the instructor, Mrs. Nelson, was introducing herself. She watched Pria, waiting for her to take her seat.

"Okay, class, as I was saying, I'm Mrs. Nelson. I've been a nurse for twenty years and an instructor here at Blue Lake Community College for five. I'd like everyone to stand up and introduce yourself. Before you complain, yes, it will take the entire class period to get to each of you, but I feel this is a valuable way to begin. Please tell me a little about yourself or why you want to be a nurse's aide."

The students looked anxious trying to think of an answer that would please Mrs. Nelson without revealing too much about themselves. There weren't any extroverts in this class. The majority of the students slid down in their chairs. Pria began pulling on her cuticles, not caring it was the wrong day. This kind of attention she detested.

"Any volunteers?"

A young man at the front of the class raised his hand.

"Wonderful, go ahead."

"Hey, my name is Caleb. I, uh, I used to have a music store. I'm taking this class so I can help a buddy of mine. He, uh, he's locked up, and I want to work at his place. Uh, I guess it's not his place." Caleb laughed while looking at the class.

"I mean he's locked up in a mental ward and I want to help him. So that's it." Caleb sat down without further comment.

Caleb's speech caught Pria's attention. His reason for becoming a nurse's aide was the same as hers. She wondered if she would be brave enough to talk to him about it after class. He seemed familiar to her, but couldn't remember why. She would observe him and try to learn more about him throughout the course of their class. Maybe she'd remember where she'd seen him.

The next person to stand up was a tall woman with short-cropped blonde hair. Clearing her voice before speaking, she appeared self-conscious and meek.

The Plucker

"Hello, my name is Claire. My children are grown up and I find I'm at a loss. I don't have any hobbies; I need something to keep me busy. My mother lived in a nursing home for the last five years of her life." Claire cleared her voice again. "I thought the aides who helped her were such wonderful people. I want to give back and do the same."

Claire returned to her seat, looked down at her hands, then up again at Mrs. Nelson, searching for her instructor's approval. Mrs. Nelson nodded at Claire then turned back to the class.

"Okay, that's exactly what I want to hear. I would like to get to know each of you and your motivation for being in this class. This is not a glamorous profession. The hours can be brutal, some of your patients will be hard to handle, and some may seem ungrateful. You need to understand the reality of the job you're training for. Now, who's next?"

It was Pria's turn to stand up and introduce herself. She clasped her hands together behind her back to keep them from traveling up to her eyebrows. She stood and faced the teacher, not the other members of her class.

"My name is Pria, spelled P-R-I-A."

Her voice was so quiet Mrs. Nelson had to interrupt and ask her to speak up.

"My name is Pria, spelled P-R-I-A. My name might sound unusual to you, that's why I've decided to tell you how to spell it. There is someone I know who is in a mental institution and I want to help him. He doesn't know that I'm doing this, but I hope that by becoming a nurse's aide I can make his life a little better."

Pria sat down, unclasped her hands, and looked out the window. She thought about George. Wondering how he could bear being locked up, confused about how his mother could do that to him.

She didn't notice Caleb staring at her.

Chapter Nine

Pria wanted to change; she wanted to stop being stuck in her obsessive daily rituals. It was time to go back to her psychiatrist, Dr. Tine.

She'd quit seeing him when she left home, thinking there was nothing wrong with her. Her little quirks, as she liked to call them, weren't hurting anyone else. They helped her move from one day to the next. But last night she'd made a decision: more spontaneity might be good for her. A shocking but enticing realization.

Monday morning after she played her guitar—after all, it was too soon to make a change—she called Dr. Tine's office. It took ten minutes of staring at her telephone to work up the nerve to call. Pria was pleased to find out he had an opening at 11 am.

Feeling hopeful, she rode the bus to his office located in a medical building downtown. During the ride she started to feel more anxious and began to wonder if it was all a mistake. Instead of plucking any part of her body, she began to scratch the top of her hands, a new behavior. What did it mean?

Standing in front of the old medical building, she remembered some of her past sessions with Dr. Tine during her childhood. He was always kind but pushed her to answer his probing questions. That proved very difficult for Pria as a child.

She didn't know why she pulled out her eyebrows. The sessions were a result of her mother's worry about Pria's constant and obsessive hair pulling, her trichotillomania.

She hoped Dr. Tine's methods were a bit gentler now. She needed his help to ease into her new life without pressure. Pria entered the building, shoring up her courage, determined to take charge of the session.

The rickety old elevators were still there, causing her to smile. The door opened and there was a familiar old man still manning his station on the elevator, still wearing his uniform and white gloves. She stepped inside, nodding to him, although there is no possible way he remembered her.

"Dr. Tine's office, please."

The Plucker

The elevator operator returned her nod, pressing the button to close the door and then selecting the correct floor for Dr. Tine's office. They rode together in silence.

Pria was a few minutes early so she sat in the outer reception area waiting for the doctor to finish with his previous patient. She'd never seen any other patients and wondered if he didn't have many or if he liked to spread out the patients throughout the day. She supposed it didn't really matter. Pria felt comfortable around him since she'd seen him before and knew that if anyone could help her, it was him.

The door to his office opened and a young man wearing a dark-colored hooded sweat jacket walked out fiddling with his smartphone, not turning back to say goodbye to the doctor. Not looking up to see where he was going. He headed straight for the door out to the elevator. While waiting for the elevator to arrive, Pria watched through the open door as he pulled the hood up over his head.

Caleb. What was he doing here?

Pria felt her heart skip a beat. Worried she was now imagining things; she wondered if he could be the hoodie guy from the bus. It seemed odd that she'd already run into the blonde at the park and now Caleb.

Pria wondered if her imagination was playing tricks on her or if the world could really be that small. Did she have a role to play in both of their lives?

The doctor's door opened, and he greeted Pria in a hearty voice.

"Hello, Pria, it's been a very long time since I've seen you. I'm very happy you decided to come back."

Dr. Tine seemed genuinely happy, smiling at Pria as she followed him into his office. He directed her to the familiar chair across his seat at the desk. It made her feel secure knowing that nothing looked different. She peeked at his bookcase—the same group of books. She looked around and saw the same pictures on his wall. Pria was back in time and liked it.

"So I'm curious, Pria, why are you here after all these years?"

Pria begin to scratch the top of her hands again, trying to gather her thoughts.

"So I'm still doing that thing that you tried to treat me for when I was little. I think I want to stop but I'm not sure."

Dr. Tine opened up his brown folder, re-reading his notes from her childhood sessions.

"You were very resistant as a child to making any changes. I thought I recalled that and now that I've re-read your notes I see that I am correct. So I want to know why you've decided to change now."

The Plucker

The dark-paneled room was silent for a few minutes while Pria gathered her thoughts. Dr. Tine didn't bother her or make her rush. Instead he fiddled with his fountain pen, looking out the window, waiting.

"It's just… I'm feeling burdened by everything I'm compelled to do. Every day I've assigned myself a task and cannot get on with my day unless I do it."

Pria stop scratching her hands and looked directly into Dr. Tine' eyes.

"In the beginning it was soothing, but now on some days it feels like a burden. The problem is, although these rituals sometimes feel more like a task than a pleasure, once I do them I feel good. Really, really good."

Dr. Tine added a fresh piece of paper to Pria's file, uncapped his fountain pen, ready to add new notes.

"I'd like you to tell me what you do each day. I need to get some idea of what you're doing on a daily basis."

"Monday, I pluck the strings on my guitar in order, beginning with the top one. Sometimes more than once, depending on my mood. But the important thing is to pluck them in order."

Pria paused for Dr. Tine's reaction.

"Don't worry about waiting for my response to each day. Please just list the rest of the week and then we'll go from there."

"Okay, then. Tuesdays I try new things, although lately I've changed my Tuesday agenda. I don't want to talk about that yet. On Wednesdays I visit my pigeons in the park and feed them. Thursdays, Fridays, and Saturdays I attend community college. My job used to be at the pickle factory but I was laid off. I tried different jobs but kept getting fired. Every other Sunday I pluck my eyebrows. On the non-plucking Sundays I rest and recover. Oh, and I bake cornbread to feed to the pigeons."

It was Dr. Tine's turn to be quiet. Scribbling, then pausing, he began to nibble on the end of the fountain pen. He started to speak a couple of times, cleared his throat, then stopped. He grabbed another sheet of paper to add to her file, attaching it to the clips at the top, trying to give himself more time to think about his response to Pria's revelations.

"Well, Pria, I have to say I'm a bit concerned at how regimented your life has become. It's normal for a person to have some routine in their life, but you seem to be addicted to it. Let me ask you this, how would you feel if this Wednesday you didn't go to the park to meet with your pigeon friends?"

Pria's eyes widened in shock. She began scratching the tops of her hands again, shifting in her seat, feeling trapped rather than safe.

The Plucker

"I can't imagine a Wednesday without my friends, Dr. Tine. I don't want to imagine Wednesdays like that! It makes me nauseous to think about not visiting them."

Pria began to hyperventilate, reminding herself of the blonde on the bus, feeling lightheaded. Close to passing out.

"I want you to take a deep breath and relax. Please try to calm down. I'm simply asking you a question, I'm not telling you to do this yet. Let me pose another question to you. What if you visited your pigeons on say, Monday instead of Wednesday? Would that feel any better?"

Pria shot up from her chair and began backing out of the room.

"Sit down, please, Pria. I need to hear your answer to my question."

"No…no, Dr. Tine, I can't imagine that! My friends need to see me on Wednesdays and only Wednesdays. If I *could* change it I would see them every day. But that wouldn't work, it would be a disaster. This is a disaster. I need…I need to go now. I don't think I'll be back."

She ran out of the room, slamming the door behind her. She pressed the down button *pigeon* times to call the elevator.

Wiping her red eyes while facing the back of the elevator, Pria tried to gather herself. Her session had proved to be more difficult than she had imagined it would be. Dr. Tine tried to be kind, but his probing questions made her feel vulnerable. She had neglected to put any tissues in her purse, which forced her to wipe her eyes with her long-sleeved shirt. Reaching the first floor, Pria dried her cheeks then walked out to face the world.

Hoping to look natural but not having a mirror to confirm her appearance, she noticed everyone kept looking at her face. Some tried to sneak a look at her while others stared openly at her red eyes, tear-streaked face, and worried demeanor.

I must look awful! Everyone knows I've been crying. I need to find a place to hide.

She left the building, looking in desperation for a quiet corner or bench to be still and calm down. While looking for sanctuary from the stares of passersby, she found a spot that looked promising down the block.

Pria ducked into a donut shop. Donuts, a comfort food for many, including Pria. The dispassionate clerk took her order for a maple bar and a cup of tea. Taking her food, she slid into a tattered booth near the back of the shop. Her anxiety lessened with each bite of maple goodness. The hot tea relaxed her, allowing her to lean back into the vinyl bench.

The Plucker

Wishing she'd brought a book with her, Pria watched the other customers. There were three people in the dark shop. A pair of teenagers sitting on opposite sides of a table, not talking or looking at one another. Both stared with rapt attention at the small glowing screens of their smartphones. The other customer sat in the last booth in the back of the shop. It was the woman from the bus. Pria now referred to her as 'the blonde' since this was the second time she'd seen her.

The blonde seemed nervous to Pria. Looking around, her eyes never settled on one thing. The woman seemed to be struggling with herself. After a few minutes of internal angst, the woman nodded to herself and became still. Pria couldn't stop staring at her. Allowing herself to take a sip of tea, Pria looked over at the blonde again. She blinked several times, then looked again.

Gone.

Pria peered under the table, thinking the woman was looking for something on the floor. Nothing. *Did I imagine her?*

Taking another sip of her tea, Pria looked at the back booth again. Still no one there. The front doorbell rang, causing Pria to turn her head. Walking in, a bit disheveled, was the blonde.

How strange. There must be a door in the back I can't see from here. Pria decided it was time to leave the shop and go home.

Staring at her hands while waiting for the bus, she felt someone walk past her. Pria looked up and saw it was Caleb. Hoodie guy. He didn't notice her, busy walking while texting.

Everyone around here is strange.

While making this observation, Pria began to scratch her forearm. It had begun tingling in the donut shop. She wanted to know what color the string would be, but resisted the urge to look. This was not the place for that.

As Pria boarded the bus, she thought about the blonde. The woman in the donut shop was the Deep Breather.

Pria recalled her last day at the florist shop. She'd broken her employer's rules by telling a caller the details of the person who'd sent flowers. The woman on the phone seemed worried and insisted on knowing the identity of the person who'd sent the bouquet. The buyer wanted to remain anonymous, but Pria no longer cared. Her boss fired her earlier that day for her obsessive plucking, and told her to leave at the end of her shift. She'd lost another job due to her compulsions.

The Plucker

She'd recognized the customer as the hoodie guy from the bus a few weeks ago. He creeped her out, wearing the same jacket and dark glasses, ashamed, not wanting to be identified. She'd felt no duty to protect his identity then.

Worried he'd sent the flowers to the blonde woman on the bus, it was her way to help. The same woman Pria saw in the donut shop today. The magical woman with the ability to go through walls.

The mystery deepened for Pria but she had no time to solve it. Her top priority was still George.

Chapter Ten

Yesterday's introductions during class drained Pria. Now that the most difficult part of being in the class was over, she was eager to begin learning. Entering the classroom, she headed to the back row but stopped when she felt a tap on her shoulder. It was Caleb, and he was smiling at her.

"Yeah, hi. I'm Caleb. Don't know if you remember me from yesterday, but, um, I kinda wanted to talk to you, P-R-I-A."

"Are you making fun of me?"

"Nah, just wanted to show you I was paying attention when you introduced yourself to the class, no offense. I think Pria is a pretty name."

"Class is going to start, so I should sit down."

Caleb's smile faltered a bit, then he regained his confidence.

The Plucker

"Okay. How about coffee after class?"

Pria's cheeks began to burn. She turned away so Caleb wouldn't see and mumbled a quick 'yes.'

The instructor began to go over the requirements for the upcoming labs. She gave the students a list of items they needed to buy, which all seemed normal to Pria. Then the instructor moved on to the physical requirements, causing Pria's ears to perk up.

Each of them must be able to lift at least fifty pounds. *No problem*, she thought. All students must keep their nails short. *No problem*, Pria thought again.

And finally, the instructor said, all students must wear short-sleeved uniform tops. Pria began to panic as she thought about her magical arms, trying to think what she could do. She didn't want to quit now. This was the work she wanted to do, but having anyone see her arms was not an option.

Pria couldn't think about Caleb's unexpected invitation; she had a bigger problem. The instructor's dress code for labs was going to be difficult for Pria to conform to. Short sleeves.

She had one week until she had to comply. One week to figure out how to hide her forearms. Her miracle. Or she'd have to quit school and give up on her dream of helping George.

Focus Pria. Stop worrying. Focus or you'll fail. Failing is not the way to solve this.

She leaned back, ready to learn about transferring a patient from a bed to a wheelchair. Her thin forearms, covered in a long-sleeved shirt, twitched. Her fingers crept inside her right sleeve, inching toward her newest string. Pria needed to release her stress.

The class break provided Pria with a chance for relief. She entered the same stall she used yesterday and rolled up her sleeve. Her hand hovered over her arm, hesitating while she chose. A small bead of sweat formed above her left eyebrow, pressure built up in her chest. Then the sound of an explosion outside her stall door.

Too late, I should have plucked sooner. How will I explain the broken glass in the bathroom?

Two minutes late after the break, Pria sat at her desk then mouthed, "I'm sorry," to her instructor.

The only student to notice her tardiness was Caleb. He nodded in her direction and smiled.

Getting off the bus at the mall, Pria found the uniform store. With no desire to spend much time there, she grabbed a plain white outfit. Pants and a short-sleeved top. The clerk inquired whether she wanted to try it on. Pria refused with a mumbled "I know my size."

"Are you sure, miss? Wouldn't it be easier to try on the uniform now? The dressing rooms are empty, it won't take long."

"No, thank you, I know my size. Just let me pay so I can leave," said Pria.

"Well, okay then," said the clerk.

Next stop was the drugstore. She found the makeup section, a strange area to her; she'd never worn makeup. Staring at the wall of beauty, brows drawn together, she felt paralyzed. A woman adorned with heavy makeup approached her.

"Need some help? I'm in charge of the makeup department in this store."

Pria stared at her, not sure how to answer. Silent moments passed, both women stuck.

"I need…I need a way to cover up a scar."

"Where's the scar? Want me to look at it?"

"No, no. It's in an…embarrassing place. I just need a way to cover it up. Is there something here I could use? Something to match my color?" Pria, self-conscious about her brown skin again.

"Oh, sure. Follow me."

Further down the aisle was a display with shades from the palest white to the darkest ebony. Her color sat there waiting for Pria. It was labeled 'Golden Brown.' A surge of joy filled her. She wasn't boring brown, she was Golden Brown.

"This special makeup is designed to cover scars, birthmarks, whatever you don't want to be seen. As a bonus, it's waterproof! Let me know if you need anything else."

"Does it cover areas that aren't smooth? I have some bumps that I'd like to hide."

"Not sure about bumps, but give it a try. If you don't like the makeup you can return it, no problem," said the sales clerk.

Pria purchased two containers of Golden Brown, excited to try it at home. She wanted to believe the clerk. Wanted to keep her miracle a secret. As she left the drugstore she had a fleeting thought: *How will my strings look covered in this stuff?*

Back at her apartment, Pria thought about the odd coffee date she'd had with Caleb after class. When she tried to shake his hand, he stepped back, saying, "Sorry, I don't touch living people."

Feeling brave, Pria asked what that meant. Caleb didn't answer; he looked everywhere but into her eyes. She kept staring at him, demanding an explanation with her silence. Pria didn't want to have coffee with someone more peculiar than her.

"So, okay, I had a problem when I was ten. Now I'm afraid to touch anyone in case the problem comes back."

"What problem?"

"It's not important, seriously, it's not. I just want to talk to you about my friend. The one in the loony bin."

"What was your problem? I think it's important for me to know if we're going to be…friends."

"Promise you won't freak out when I tell you," said Caleb.

"I'll try, that's all I can promise."

"Well, okay, I did something pretty bad when I was ten. I mean, it wasn't planned or anything, but he deserved it."

"What are you talking about, Caleb? Who deserved what?"

"My old man, my father. He was cruel. I…well, I killed him."

They stared at one another for several seconds before Pria could respond.

"I don't know, Caleb, you seem to have some issues I'm not comfortable with. Maybe this is a bad idea. And your friend is not in a loony bin. No one says that. Unless they are uncaring."

"Okay, sorry. I'm nervous. I don't talk to many girls. This will take a few minutes. I want to compare notes because I have a feeling we have the same friend. His name is George."

Pria didn't trust Caleb. If he killed once—and she wasn't sure if it was only once—why should she think he wouldn't have the same urge now? She wondered if this was a trick. How is it possible they knew the same person? She considered her next move.

"No, I don't know any George. You're mistaken. I need to leave. I have to pick up my supplies for lab. Please don't bother me again."

Amazed with herself for this new ability to lie, she turned before Caleb could answer, feeling her body shake with fear and confusion. Tempted to turn and see if he followed, she forced herself to keep looking ahead. As the door to the coffee shop closed, the sound of breaking glass echoed out onto the sidewalk. Pria smiled.

That should keep that freak away from me.

The Plucker

Pria smiled at her solution to the problem of Caleb and began to concentrate on her arms. The directions on the jar seemed simple. Apply and let it dry before putting any clothing over the area.

She opened a jar of the Golden Brown makeup, dipping her fingers into the viscous cream. She spread it onto a small patch of skin on top of one of the strings. The string's color changed, blending into her skin. Although the color matched, the makeup didn't hide the strings. Now she looked like she had long, golden-brown hairs growing in sporadic patches.

Maybe it won't be noticeable. Maybe my new ability to lie includes lying to myself.

Not wanting to feel discouraged, Pria put on the short-sleeved uniform top. Hideous. She knew she looked freakish. The only solution would be to shave or pluck all of her strings.

I could shave my arms, but it would be an act of destruction. The destruction of my real self. As much as I want to help George I can't be false to myself.

Pria washed the makeup off her arm, then rolled her sleeves down to protect her miracle. She delayed her decision and decided to escape with one of her favorite romantic movies.

The pleasure she felt after watching her beloved film eluded her. Pria obsessed over what to do about her arms. Her pink razor beckoned from her tiny bathroom, offering a quick solution. Reversible if she chose to answer the siren call of the gleaming double blade, but something she'd live with for days. Warned by her prickling scalp to relax, Pria dreaded the chore of cleaning broken glass in her apartment if she lost control. Delicate brown fingers tugged on a blue string begging for attention.

I can't make a decision tonight. My deadline will be tomorrow morning, I have to sleep and let my dreams tell me what to do.

That evening Pria dreamt many odd things. No hair anywhere on her body, blue eyes not brown, peach-hued skin, no longer dark. An altered Pria flew over the city unashamed of her nakedness. The next dream showed her sitting on her bench at the park, selling the string on her arms. The pigeons she'd befriended delivered the strings to her buyers.

The morning didn't bring any resolution, instead it handed Pria dread. She couldn't delay her life trying to figure out the best way to proceed.

Shave her arms and become an aide, but lose her sense of specialness? Could she sacrifice that for her friend George, or was there another solution?

The Plucker

She'd sworn to never go back to Dr. Tine, but she needed someone to talk to. Someone who might be able to guide her without judgment. Not a task her parents were up to. Judgment was a part of their DNA.

As the phone rang for Dr. Tine's office, Pria curled her fingers around a clump of hair and yanked it out. No subtlety today, she needed a quick brutal charge of adrenaline to get through this call.

Appointment made, she counted the number of days until she would see Dr. Tine. Three days of indecision, seventy-two hours of anxiety, four thousand three hundred twenty minutes of stress.

Chapter Eleven

Pria entered the old medical building desperate for help. The ancient elevator operator was there again, which proved to be as comforting as when she last visited Dr. Tine. Knowing she might be making some changes, it felt good to see something remain the same.

Pria waited in the reception area until it was time for her appointment. Nervous. She tried to imagine a life free of compulsions. Her thoughts were interrupted when Dr. Tine opened his door and ushered her into his office.

Dr. Tine remained standing when Pria entered the room and greeted her with a stiff smile. Seemingly unsure about what to expect after their last session, he let her take the lead this time.

"Nice to see you again, Pria. I do have to admit I was rather surprised you made another appointment after the way you ended our last session."

"I want to apologize about last time, Dr. Tine. I guess I wasn't ready for change at that point, and what you were suggesting frightened me. But I'm back and need your advice about something I've been working on. I now know I need the help of a professional to do this. I can't go this alone."

Dr. Tine gestured toward the chair across from his desk and remained silent until Pria sat down.

"You know my purpose is to help my patients, so please go ahead and explain what it is I can do for you. I won't ask any questions until you finish, and then perhaps we can discuss some possible solutions. Do you agree, Pria?"

"Yes, I do, and I promise I won't run away. I need to solve my dilemma and will give your ideas a chance."

Pria explained her wish to meet up with her childhood friend, George, and her plan to become a nurse's aide. She pointed out her double dilemma: should she go on with the plan to become an aide and work in the mental hospital George resides in? And if so, how could she force herself to shave or pluck her arms?

She leaned back in her chair, relieved to give her burden to Dr. Tine. The back of her head tingled but she resisted the urge to pull her hair, resting her hands on her lap. Waiting.

Hesitant to rush in with a solution, Dr. Tine shuffled the papers on his desk. He walked over to his bookshelf to give himself time to think. With a curt nod of his head, he signaled his readiness to proceed.

"Let's start with your desire to see your old friend. Do you have romantic feelings for him?"

Pria's cheeks began to redden.

"No, that's not the reason, Dr. Tine. He's someone from my childhood that I want to reconnect with. George was my only friend." The last part whispered to herself.

"Are you telling me you two played together? Was there an actual friendship?" Dr. Tine looked skeptical.

"Played together? It depends on your definition of played together."

"No, it doesn't, Pria. You need to tell me the truth, no fantasies."

"Okay, we never played together, but I could tell he liked me. Or rather, I could tell he didn't think I was strange. George never sneered at me, or teased me. He was the only one."

"Then what you're saying is you *wish* George was your friend. From your description he doesn't seem to be the kind of person who has a lot of people in his life. Am I correct in this assumption?'

"It wasn't his fault! His mother was, and still is, cruel. She only loves herself. How could he have relationships with anyone? How?"

Pria felt tears brimming, aching to flow down her cheeks. Threatening to force her to feel emotions long repressed.

"Calm down, I'm not saying anything you don't already know," said Dr. Tine. "The real question to you is why you have this need to reconnect with George. What is your motivation? Do you think he'll cure you of your obsessive behaviors?"

"I'm lonely, Dr. Tine. There, you've made me say it. I don't have any friends; people think I'm odd. I don't talk to anyone unless they speak to me first. My favorite time is with my pigeons on Wednesdays. So I guess I'm a freak!"

The teardrops won their battle with gravity, rolling down her cheeks. Pria noticed the same relief she experienced while plucking. Her shoulders relaxed, and for the first time since early childhood, a sense of calm enveloped her.

"I don't think you're a freak. You have some issues, but I don't know anyone who doesn't. Now that you've opened up to me about your reason for befriending George, we can move on."

Dr. Tine started to reach out and pat Pria's hand, changed his mind, and sat back. Instead he began to pick at his cuticles, then stopped when he realized what he was doing.

Pria and Dr. Tine discussed whether training to become an aide was a good idea. After a few minutes they came to an agreement. Although Pria's plan was kind, it wasn't what would make her happy. Instead, Dr. Tine suggested she visit George. On a Wednesday.

Relieved her arms were safe, Pria left the doctor's office happy.

The entrance to George's residence intimidated Pria. No, it wasn't his home, it was a hospital. Not intended for patients sick with a disease of the body, but rather of the mind. Her George lived here. Institutionalized by an uncaring, selfish mother.

Dr. Tine had agreed to meet her there on the Wednesday following her appointment with him. That day of the week was for her pigeon friends; this would be the first time since she'd begun her visits that she'd miss her time with them in the park. By the time she traveled to and from the hospital by bus and visited with George, the day would be nearly over.

Aware of her dilemma when he proposed the day for her visit to George, Dr. Tine was hoping a change in one of her routines would help Pria begin to break free of her compulsions.

Maybe I can visit them after I see George. It will be dark, but they'll be so worried if I don't show up. Hungry too. What if they think I've deserted them?

Deep breaths and plucked cuticles calmed Pria down before she stepped through the scarred oak doors of the hospital. The nurse's station just inside marked the beginning of her journey into her friend's curious reality.

"May I help you?" said an older nurse reading a chart.

Pria stood still, unsure how to proceed.

"May I help you, young lady?" This time the nurse looked at Pria instead of her pile of papers.

"I'm here to meet up with Dr. Tine. He said he'd be here at 11 am."

"What's your name?"

"It's Pria. P-R-I-A."

"Okay, I found your name. He called to say he would be about fifteen minutes late this morning. Have a seat. Want any tea or coffee?"

"Um, no, thank you. But is there a restroom I can use?"

"Down the hall, second door on the right."

The far stall seemed safe from prying eyes. She slid the latch on the door, continuing the motion up her arm to push up her sleeve. Pausing over her arm, Pria took a few seconds to choose the perfect string for this situation. The longest blue string sacrificed in celebration.

Back at the waiting area, Pria took a shallow breath, the air leaving her mouth in a turbulent cloud of fear. This was the day she'd been waiting for; she was so close to seeing George. Confused by her sense of dread, she took deeper breaths to calm herself before sitting.

"Pria?" said the nurse. "Dr. Tine called to let us know he's ready for you. Just go down this hall behind us and meet him in his office. His name is on the door."

"He has an office here? I didn't know that. Okay, thanks for telling me."

Pria found the office, then knocked. After Dr. Tine told her to come in she walked into his hospital office.

It looked nothing like his other one. It was stark and empty of any personal effects. The metal desk and chairs a shocking contrast to the wood and warmth of his primary workspace. Pria's scalp began to tingle.

"Are you ready for this, Pria?" said Dr. Tine.

"I need to go to the bathroom, please. I'll be right back."

The Plucker

Pria rushed from the sterile room and headed to the comfort of the bathroom stall. Control, she needed to control her emotions. Not bothering to check if the restroom was empty, Pria grabbed a chunk of hair from the ever-increasing bald spot under the curtain of hair at the back of her head. She yanked, yelped with pain, then shuddered in relief. Now she felt ready.

"Sorry about that, Dr. Tine," she said upon returning. "I think I have a nervous stomach. I'm ready. Let's go."

Neither spoke during the short walk to the elevators. George's room was on the 21st floor. Pria thought it was a good sign his floor was *pigeon*. Her favorite number.

An attendant waited outside the door to George's room. He nodded to Dr. Tine, then raised his eyebrows to ask if they were going in.

"No, Mark," said Dr. Tine. "We need to observe George for a few minutes first. I'll call you if we need you, thanks."

During this brief interaction, Pria stood at the two-way mirror, staring into the room. George sat at a small metal table talking to his companion. She'd heard about Eve from Lilith, George's bitter mother, but wasn't prepared to see 'her.'

Eve was little more than a doll. A black wig sat on the mannequin head, the body dressed in an old blue dress. Pria knew the dress covered a rudimentary robot body.

The look on George's face showed the love he had for his companion. They were having a conversation, drinking tea, and laughing. Pria looked with longing at their happiness and wanted the same thing for herself.

"Let's talk to him, Dr. Tine."

The doctor rang for Mark and requested he unlock the door.

"Are you sure, Dr. Tine?" asked Mark.

"Yes, but please stay outside in case we need to leave right away."

Dr. Tine walked in first and greeted George and Eve. He motioned for Pria to come inside.

"Hi, George. Do you remember me? We went to elementary school together." Pria looked from George to Eve, unsure how to react.

George looked at Pria without any sign of recognition. Then he began to smile and nod his head.

"Oh, yeah, we were in the same class for a few years. I remember you now. Eve, this is…what was your name?"

"It's Pria. P-R-I-A."

"Oh yeah, Pria. Funny name."

"How are you, George?" asked Pria. "Do you like it here?"

George looked at Eve, whispered something to her, then replied, "Sure, we love it here!"

"Okay then, it was nice seeing you. Goodbye, George. I do hope you are happy. Nice to meet you, Eve."

Pria turned to leave the room, not looking back at the odd couple sitting at the table in their own fantasy world.

Back in Dr. Tine's office, he asked her to sit.

"Are you all right, Pria?"

"That was a very strange meeting, but yes, I'm okay."

"Do you want to visit George again?" asked Dr. Tine.

"No, I've seen enough. There's nothing I can do for him. I need to work on my own life."

About to stand up and leave, Dr. Tine asked her to wait a moment.

"Do you want to continue with therapy? I know I could help you further."

Pria rubbed her arms and thought about his offer. After today's experience, she knew he could help her.

"I'll see you next Tuesday, Dr. Tine.

Epilogue

"Eve, did you like Pria?"

Eve turned to George, looking at him with her unchanging blue eyes.

"Pria? She seemed nice. Should I be jealous?" Her flirtatious giggle was directed at George.

"No worries, she was a girl I went to school with. We never even talked. I don't know why she came here, but it was nice to see someone from my old neighborhood. Makes me miss my closet. Hey, did I ever tell you about my closet? I used to read in there and keep my collections of things on the shelves."

"Yes, silly, I know all about your special closet."

"Well, did I ever tell you about Caleb?"

"Yes, Georgie, but I like hearing you talk. Go ahead."

Eve's fixed expression managed to show her devotion to George. In his eyes, she was smiling.

"He's my best friend in the whole wide world. We liked to dumpster dive together to find treasures like the teeth I used to make a necklace for my mother. One of our favorite places to collect was in the dumpster behind the Hillcrest Medical Center."

George frowned as he pictured the shock on Lilith's face when he presented her with his handmade Mother's Day gift.

"Then when he opened his little store, he gave both of us jobs. Too bad he had to close it."

"Yes, Georgie, that was sad. But don't forget, he visited us a few weeks ago."

"I wonder what he's doing now? Maybe we'll see him again."

"Maybe, Georgie. Maybe."

Mark the attendant opened the door to George's room.

"It's time for your medication."

George nodded, knowing he'd hide his pills under his tongue. Like he always did.

Author's Note

The characters Pria, George, and Caleb, first appeared in my book:

"Spilt Milk: A Collection of Stories"

Within these pages you will meet an array of characters. Choices are made that will change lives. Are they right or wrong?

You decide.

Each brief story deliberately distills a life's essence. Welcome to Modern Gothic stories that are droll, horrific, and thought provoking.

Caleb, unwanted, neglected, now grown
George, a child who collects things
Cinderella's stepmother in therapy
Jared, baptized in a coffee world
A paraplegic finds her true life
A mother lost in her torn past
And six others

If you want to know more about the 'blonde' that Pria encounters throughout this book, she is featured in "Curious Reality", the first book in the *World of Spilt Milk*.

I hope you enjoyed reading *The Plucker*. If so, please consider leaving a review on Amazon and Goodreads. Thank you very much.

Sign up for my newsletter, www.dkcassidy.com/ newsletter, for updates on new books, freebies, and interesting information. I promise never to spam you.

Cheers!
D.K. Cassidy

Acknowledgments

To friends, family, and fans that continue to cheer me on, I am ever grateful.

To my editor Crystal Watanabe, thank you for helping me refine my voice.

About the Author

D.K. Cassidy has been scribbling stories since she was a child and loves to write in various genres including Magical Realism, Modern Gothic, Science Fiction, and Literary Fiction. Her goal? Messing with your mind by transforming the voices in her head into odd stories.

D.K. Cassidy lives in the Pacific Northwest with her greatest fans: her husband Mark, twin sons Aidan and Jared, and three cats. When not writing, she loves to travel, run, use the Oxford comma, and of course read!

If you like her work please follow her:
DKCassidy.com
@moongie